SEVENTEEN AND TURNING INTO A NON-MORMON SECULAR HUMANIST ZOMBIE

Also by Scott Erickson

BOOKS

The Navy Girl Book

The Diary of Amy, the 14-Year-Old Girl Who Saved the Earth

The Best of Reality Ranch

NOVELLAS

B-Movie Mash-Up: Gastropods of Terror And How to Get a Head in Real Estate

Invasion of the Dumb Snatchers

SEVENTEEN AND TURNING INTO A NON-MORMON SECULAR HUMANIST ZOMBIE

SCOTT ERICKSON

Copyright 2016 © by Scott Erickson

All rights reserved. No part of this book may be reproduced or transmitted in any form or by any means, electronic or mechanical, including photocopying, recording, or by any information storage and retrieval system, without the written consent of the publisher, except in the case of brief quotations embodied in critical articles and reviews.

This is a work of fiction. All names, characters and incidents are the products of the authors' imagination. Where the names of actual locations or corporate entities appear, they are for fictional purposes and do not constitute assertions of fact. Any resemblance to real events or persons, living or dead, is coincidental.

ISBN: 978-0-9898311-5-4

Published in the United States of America
by Azaria Press

CHAPTER 1

Janet had just gotten off the plane in Duluth, Minnesota, when her cell phone rang. It was her father—*again*—calling from St. George, a Mormon stronghold in the desert of southern Utah where she had lived for all of her seventeen years.

She dreaded taking the call, for she feared it would go just as badly as the other calls. If only...if only she could convince him that they were wrong. Why didn't he believe her...his own daughter...his own flesh and blood? And also tears. And how there had been tears, as a result her crying, which she had been doing so much of lately...so much.

She considered the expression "my own flesh and blood" and concluded, using her mind, that it was silly. *A little bit of his sperm went into my mother's special place seventeen years ago*, she thought to herself. *And only one sperm cell got the whole thing going. How does that tiny contribution make me his 'flesh and blood'?*

She grew annoyed at the cell phone's incessant ring tone of the Carpenter's *On Top of the World*, and finally answered.

"Hello daddy," she said, brushing aside her sensible brown hair. Then added an annoyed, "Again!"

"How is my little pumpkin-eater doing? I've been so worried! I haven't talked to you in—"

"Twenty minutes!" she broke in. "Daddy, don't you trust me? I mean, I'm seventeen years old. I'm not going to get into trouble in twenty minutes!"

"Well, Janet," he answered sternly, "I left you alone once, and then—"

"Daddy!" she cried, tears shooting all over the place, "It didn't happen that way! Why don't you believe me! I'm your own...well..."

"Flesh and blood!" he screamed.

"You know, I was thinking about that whole 'flesh and blood' thing," she said. "Scientifically speaking, it's totally bogus. I mean, it was only one sperm cell."

"No!" he stopped her, "I can't hear any of this *sacrilege!*"

"Oh daddy, really!" she laughed. "The concept of *sacrilege* is irrelevant to a secular humanist."

"I can't believe that my own daughter—my little Janet the pumpkin-eater—has become a *secular humanist!* I've been praying for your soul! I'm praying right now!"

Over the phone she could hear the cartilage in his kneecaps snapping.

"Oh, daddy," she said, "you take all that 'religion stuff' so seriously. I mean, it's not as if your eternal life depended on it!"

"Oh Sweet Jesus, how can you say that?" he cried. "My own flesh and blood!"

"Well actually, daddy, since the human body completely replaces itself every seven years, that sperm cell is long gone by now."

"Now you listen to me, young lady! Unless you repent for your sins, you cannot enter the gates of Heaven."

"Daddy!" she shrieked, her tears shooting probably ten feet. "I told you it was all a misunderstanding! Why don't you believe me? *Why???* Oh, I want to die! I want to crawl under a rock and die!"

"Janet, you don't mean that! You're being a—"

"I am *not* being a drama addict!"

"Janet!"

"I want to die under a rock made of obsidian—dark and hard like my despair. I'd be okay with crawling under limestone to die, if that's all that's available. But the point is that I want to die! I want to crawl under a rock and die! I want to feel death enter me and put an end to my miserable existence!"

Suddenly, the voice of Karen Carpenter broke in: *I'm on the top of the world / looking down on creation.*

"Oh, got another call. Bye daddy!...Hello? Oh, you're from the camp?...Yes, I'm here at the airport...Your van will be here in a few minutes?...Great! Oh, by the way, it was all a misunderstanding...What do you mean 'that's what they all say'?"

For two hours the van headed north into the North Woods of Northern Minnesota in the direction of the North Star toward the North Pole. For the last hour she had seen no sign of human civilization, just towering green woody things she assumed were trees. Having lived in St. George her entire life, she had only seen photographs of trees.

The driver was a healthy-looking woman in her mid-20s with a shaved head. She had a mellow "Mona Lisa" smile, like she thought she knew the secret of life but didn't really know but didn't care that she didn't really know. The ride was silent, void of conversation.

Life wasn't fair, Janet thought. *How could a nice young teenager's life be destroyed for no good reason? She had done nothing wrong, and yet she was being punished. Why? What about the concept of as you sow, so shall you reap? What about karma? Yeah, what's up with that, all you people who believe in those things? Is life—and by extension, the universe—rational? Or is everything all topsy-turvy? Is life a cosmic joke? Or just a plain old 'knock-knock' joke?*

Knock-knock, who's there?

It's the Meaning of Life.
The Meaning of Life, who?
The Meaning of Life that doesn't exist, Hahaha!

Janet's mind grew still, unable to penetrate the same profound questions that the world's greatest living philosophers have been unable answer. Also the world's greatest dead philosophers. Unless the dead philosophers know the answer but can't tell us because they're dead.

She gazed out the window, watching the endless forest of tall woody things flow past the window. Gosh, there were lots of them. So different from St. George!

They arrived at a clearing in the trees and a large sign that read: "Lake Wichiganawaneehoohaw Wayward Youth Recovery Camp." There was a large rustic lodge building, and rows of rustic log cabins. She'd never seen anything like it, because Utah had banned the concept of "rustic" in 1963. Just saying the word *rustic* in public carried the same penalty as spitting on the sidewalk.

The van pulled beside a body of water that she assumed was Lake Wichiganawaneehoohaw. She reasoned, using her mind, that it would make no sense to call it "Lake Wichiganawaneehoohaw Wayward Youth Recovery Camp" if it was located along the shore of Lake Titchowinininhagoc. But then, she was learning that the world didn't always make sense. Oh, how she was learning that!

The water was beautiful. She wondered if it was wet. Having lived in St. George her entire life, she had only seen photographs of water.

The van screeched to a stop, even though the parking lot was gravel. Entranced by the lake, Janet was oblivious to the inappropriate sound effects and headed toward the deep blue water. After hitting her face on the van window, she decided it would be helpful to first open the door.

The water was mesmerizing. She was fascinated by the ripples...so much like Ruffles® potato chips. She was drawn to the water as a moth is drawn to a flame, except she was not a moth and water puts out flames so that metaphor doesn't really apply very well.

She walked out onto a wooden dock, alongside which were tied several "Lake Wichiganawaneehoohaw Wayward Youth Recovery Camp" canoes. She was unaccustomed to the effect of the rippling water and felt slightly queasy. She found herself wishing that for lunch she'd eaten something besides a quart of sauerkraut.

She glanced into the watery depths and spotted something moving—alive! It looked to her like a strange-looking underwater dog, except it had no fur and was long like a snake and had fins. Recall that she had never been outside of St. George.

"Hi, puppy!" she called, waving. "You sure can hold your breath a long time. Hey, what happened to your paws?"

"Hey dere!" boomed an angry Swedish voice. "Be careful dere, ya?"

The sudden voice startled Janet, and the Swedish accent made her think of windmills, which makes no sense at all. She nearly lost her balance and fell off the dock onto a duck. When she composed herself and turned around, she was shocked to see that the angry Swedish voice had come from a red-cheeked teenage boy with blonde hair and piercing blue eyes.

A defiant Janet looked him in the piercing blue eyes. "Why don't you leave me alone? I was just saying hi to the puppy!"

"Uf-da!" he said, rolling his piercing blue eyes in disgust. "Looks like we gots us anoder city slicker dot tinks dey know everyting!"

Strange, thought Janet, *that out of this teenage boy should emerge language that sounded like it was from an old man. Who uses expressions like "city slicker" anymore?*

Continuing the defiant attitude popularized by Janet three paragraphs ago, she retorted, "Just because I'm from St. George, Utah doesn't mean I'm out-of-touch with life in rural Northern Minnesota! It's just that I've never actually *seen* an underwater puppy—only photographs."

"Dot dere ain't no *puppy*!" he said, pointing to the underwater puppy. "Dot dere is what you call a *Nordern Pike*. Fierce ting it is! It'll take your fingers clean off, so be careful, ya?"

"Really?" said Janet. "A *Northern Pike?* I've never heard of such a breed."

"Uf-da!" he cried in disgust, although not rolling his piercing blue eyes this time. "I been puttin' up wit dis kinda ting for too long. Everyting has gone to heck since the 80s!"

"The 80s! Oh, I just *love* 80s music," gushed Janet. *"Her name is Rio and she dances on the sand / Just like that river twisting through a dusty land / And when she shines she really shows you all she can."*

"Huh?" he said. "I don' know what yur talkin' about."

"What?" replied a shocked Janet. "How can you not know that one?"

"You young whippersnapper!" he shouted. "Youse all da same, buncha darned city-slicker know-it-alls!"

"Oh yeah?!" yelled Janet, oozing contempt. "In a totally irrational reply, I just want you to know that what they said happened isn't true! Not at all! It was a tragic misunderstanding! Also, I have no idea why I'm telling you any of this, unless it's because underneath my superficial anger toward you I'm actually attracted, and my fear of the implications is causing me to push you away."

Janet thought to herself: *The nerve! Just because he's from a progressive country that provides universal health care to all its citizens, he thinks he's so smart!*

"Act your age, not your shoe size!" is all she could think to say.

He threw up his hands in disgust and stormed off, leaving Janet alone with her thoughts. It suddenly struck her how this whole situation was so *surreal*. Here she was, a decidedly non-wayward teenage girl in a camp for wayward youth, being punished for something she never did, being told to recover from something she never even covered.

She gazed out upon the calming blue waters. Despite that rude Swedish boy, she thought she might like it here. After the desert heat of St. George, she was refreshed by the moist coolness of the North Woods, comforted by those woody green things sticking up all over the place.

Suddenly she remembered what she had been hoping to forget...hoping upon hope that it wasn't true, that it was all a weird dream from which she would soon awaken. Suddenly it came rushing back to her consciousness: She was turning into a zombie!

CHAPTER 2

She sat down on the dock. Or rather, the sudden remembering made her fall down on the dock. She gazed into the wavy ripples of the blue water, which made her mind get wavy, until everything got wavy. This indicated she was having a flashback.

Turning into a zombie. At first she thought the doctor was joking, especially since he broke the news while he was juggling hamsters.

Janet had been feeling "out of sorts" for months. She tried explaining to her father, but he misheard and thought she said "out of shorts" which led to a really stupid conversation.

First there were the headaches. Then the occasional uncontrollable drooling. Then the unquenchable hunger for human flesh.

Her father reasoned, "This is all because of your decision to become a vegetarian. A couple of nice juicy steaks will fix you up just fine!"

"That would be awesome daddy," she answered, "As long as they're steaks made from *people*."

Also, Janet's two best friends had recently turned into zombies.

It was not a pretty scene. They were at the mall, shopping for jeans at Banana Republic. Britney had emerged from the dressing room breathing heavily with her hair mussed, followed closely by the stock boy who ran into the back of the store while buckling his belt.

"Ohmigod!" she said, rearranging her disordered clothes, "I *told* you these jeans made me look hot! José took one look and couldn't resist doing me in the dressing room!"

"Wow!" said Tiffany. "Do they have those in, like, *my size?*"

Janet broke in, responsible as always, "We don't have *time*, Tiffany! We'll be late for Tai Chi class!"

"Oh, Janet!" complained Tiffany. "You're always so darned *responsible!*"

"Seriously, you guys!" complained Janet, brushing aside her sensible brown hair. "I don't want to be late. And by the way, Britney, what do you mean by José 'doing you'?"

But before Britney could answer, she got a strange look on her face. Her eyes glazed over. Her skin took on an ashen gray pallor. Then she began drooling.

"Oh, Britney!" said Tiffany, "I *told* you not to get a corn dog at the food court!"

Suddenly, Britney took a deep bite out of Tiffany's throat. Then she tore off Tiffany's left arm and violently gnawed at it.

Almost instantly, Tiffany's face took on the same weird gray pallor and strange expression. Then she began drooling.

Then José appeared. "Watch out for the merchandise!" he yelled. "If you get any guts on it, I have to put it on sale!"

Britney shrieked, "Brains! Brains!" then twisted José's head off his body.

Janet grew discouraged. "Look you guys," she said, "I hope you don't think I'm going to use my dad's credit card to pay for your mess."

Checking her watch, she added, "Oh! Tai Chi class! I'll meet up with you guys later. Bye!"

Janet had explained all this to the doctor, who listened while keeping a growing number of plates spinning atop flexible wands.

"Yes, that's somewhat interesting," he said, "but has anything *unusual* happened to you lately?"

"Unusual?" asked Janet. "Like what?"

"Well, let me see," said the doctor before blowing up a balloon, then popping it to reveal a dove which proceeded to fly into the wall. "For example, have any of your boyfriends gotten you pregnant recently?"

Janet's face grew beet red, even though she didn't like beets. "No, doctor, of course not!" she said in a panicked voice. "I don't even *have* a boyfriend! In fact, I'm still a virgin."

The doctor's plates all crashed to the floor and the doctor fell out of his chair.

"Doctor!" complained Janet, "Exactly *what* are you implying?"

Just at that moment, Janet noticed his diploma: *Doctor of Magic and Juggling, available for corporate functions, bar mitzvahs, and parties.*

The party! Suddenly she remembered. Then things got fuzzy again, indicating that she was having a flashback within the flashback. She began leaving a trail of breadcrumbs so later she could follow her way back to the present.

The party was the day before the mall incident. Janet didn't want to go, but Britney and Tiffany had shamed her into it.

"What's the matter, Janet," sniffed Britney, "are you afraid you might loosen up and have *fun?*"

"Oh no, Janet doesn't want to have *fun*," Tiffany added sarcastically. "She'd rather be a *secular humanist*."

"Okay, that does it!" said Janet, with a defiant toss of her sensible brown hair, "I'll show *you* that I know how to have fun, gosh darn it!"

The party was at a suburban home of a teen whose strict Mormon parents had left for a weekend prayer conference in Las Vegas. There must have been a hundred teenagers there, drinking not-legal-for-teenager beverages and talking loudly, their conversations peppered with salty language as if they were using words to season their scrambled eggs. Couples would occasionally run off to a bedroom and return an hour later, smiling in blissful exhaustion after some engaging non-fiction reading, Janet assumed.

Janet was too naïve to realize that the "punch" contained nothing of the kind. "This punch is *weird*," she said, scrunching her face with displeasure. "This doesn't taste like any fruit I've ever heard of."

The next thing she remembered, many hours later, is sitting on a bedroom floor in a circle of people, playing a game called "spin the bottle," except that nobody could find a bottle. Someone was saying, "It's your turn, Janet! Spin the pickle!"

A chorus of voices echoed, "Spin the pickle! Spin the pickle!"

Her mind was spinning, and the room was spinning, and suddenly a pickle was also spinning. It was almost as if everything was spinning. Actually, it was exactly as if everything was spinning.

'Round and 'round went the pickle, which reminded Janet of a frog, if the frog had been rolled into a cigar shape and had the front and back legs removed. When the pickle finally stopped spinning, one end point toward her and the other end pointed toward...*a boy!*

Paralyzed by confusion and punch, she was helpless as the boy dragged her off into the closet, her ankles sliding along the carpet.

Oh my goodness! she thought. *My ankles are naked!*

The boy closed the closet door behind them, then whispered to Janet, "Don't worry, I'm not going to do any weird sex stuff to you. This might sound weird, but I'm saving myself for after I'm not a virgin."

"That pickle reminded me of a frog," replied Janet. It was the punch talking.

"All I want," said the boy, beginning to salivate, "is a little *nibble.*"

Then he bit her shoulder.

Then all hell broke loose. Sirens wailed. Blinding lights flashed through the windows. Doors came crashing down. A loud voice yelled through a megaphone, "HOLD IT RIGHT THERE, WE HAVE YOU SURROUNDED!"

The headline in the next day's St. George Spectrum announced: "Teens Nabbed in Booze-Fueled Cannibalistic Drug Orgy."

Typical media hyperbole, thought Janet, reading the article while rubbing the painful shoulder bite. *It was just a little game of "spin the pickle" that got out of hand.*

The weird thing—which she learned after talking to Britney and Tiffany later on—is that they had also been subjected to "a little nibble" courtesy of that strange boy.

She continued reading the newspaper, and noticed another news item: "And in a totally unrelated story, strange boy runs amuck after transformation into flesh-eating zombie."

"I see," said the doctor, bringing Janet back to flashback #1. "That's somewhat interesting, but what I want to know is: How did all these breadcrumbs get into my office?"

"Oh doctor," she said, tears welling up, "you must believe me! It was all a misunderstanding! But my father doesn't believe me. He's threatening to send me off to some wayward teen camp to punish me."

"Well, I believe he has the legal right to do that."

"But I didn't do anything wrong!" she cried, tears shooting all over the floor and soaking the breadcrumbs.

"Well, Janet," said the doctor, "I have good news and bad news. Which would you like first?"

As Janet pondered, the doctor snacked on a few of the breadcrumbs.

"Salty!" he said.

"Oh doctor," Janet pleaded, "get the bad news over with first, so we can end with something positive."

"Okey-doke," he said, slicing open an orange to reveal a large egg. "The bad news is that you are turning into a zombie."

"Oh, is that *all?*" said a relieved Janet. "Good thing we caught it in time. Just shoot me up with the anti-zombie vaccine or antibiotics or whatever."

"Um...rather than reply to that directly, let's turn our attention to the *good* news," said the doctor, breaking open the egg to reveal a furry yellow chick. "You have a great opportunity here to live it up, for a little while. Take up smoking. Do drugs. Have unprotected sex with HIV-positive heroin addicts. Also, don't bother contributing to a retirement plan or worrying about whether the Social Security system will remain viable."

"Doctor, what are you saying?" replied Janet nervously, her face turning white as a parsnip, even though she didn't like parsnips, "Are you trying to tell me there's *no cure?*"

"Well, there are two cures for zombies: Cut off the head or smash the brains."

"Oh, this is *horrible!*" cried Janet, streams of tears shooting out and splashing off the wall. "I've had my entire future taken away from me. I'll never see Europe, never go skydiving, never play linebacker for the Denver Broncos." She grew wistful, and added, "I'll never have a family. I'll never get married. And what about *sex?*"

"No thanks," said the doctor. "You're only seventeen. Also, I generally avoid having sex with zombies."

"But I'm not a zombie yet!"

"Yes, and that's what's puzzling. Your friends became zombies soon after being bitten. Yet with you it's been over a month and you're only starting to have zombie symptoms. I have no idea why, unless it's because your mallrat friends were practically zombies already, mentally speaking. In other words, perhaps there's a correlation between intelligence and resistance to the onset of the zombie transformation?"

"That might be true," mused Janet. "I have an IQ of 140, and Britney and Tiffany were too low to register, except for the shopping portion of the test."

"Interesting hypothesis, but we can't be sure. Believe it or not, almost no medical research has been conducted on this subject."

"Why not?"

"Well, I believe the reasoning is that medical research is difficult, time-consuming, and very expensive, whereas smashing the head with a shovel is quick and easy."

Suddenly, it was all clear to Janet. She knew what had to be done.

"Doctor," said Janet. "It's suddenly all clear to me. I know what has to be done."

"I know," replied the doctor, "I heard the narrator."

"I'm not going to let it happen to me, which could cause me to impose the same fate upon someone else. Therefore, I am prepared to take my own life. I refuse to pass on this suffering; I refuse to deprive others of the future that I have been deprived of."

"Wow, that's really noble of you."

"I mean," clarified Janet, "I wouldn't be depriving them of *my* future. I mean, they have a whole different future I would be depriving them of. I just want to make sure I'm being clear."

"Well it's been great knowing you, Janet. Feel free to borrow my shovel, but can I ask as a courtesy that you smash your brains outside my office? Nothing personal, it's just that I had the carpet shampooed last week. Oh, and if you could pay for this appointment at this time I'd really appreciate it."

"Um, doctor? That's not what you're supposed to say."

"Oh—I forgot to say that I accept all major credit cards."

"No!" said Janet. "What you're *supposed* to say is: *Janet, it's vital for you to carry on. Perhaps medical science can learn from you the secret of how to halt the zombie transformation. Perhaps medical science can learn the secret, and turn it into a very expensive drug that will earn billions of dollars for the pharmaceutical industry.*"

"Oh yeah," said the doctor. "What you said."

"Also, this story would end right here. Pretty short story arc, and not emotionally fulfilling."

"Yes!" exclaimed the doctor. "And we'd never know what happens between you and that odd

Swedish boy along the shore of Lake Wichiganawaneehoohaw in Northern Minnesota."

"Doctor!" shouted Janet. "You can't know about that! All that takes place in the future! We're still in flashback #1!"

"Are we? I can't tell. The narrative structure has gone totally catawampus."

Janet suddenly noticed the breadcrumbs were gone. "Oh no! You ate all my breadcrumbs! Now I'll *never* find my way back to the present!"

"Wait a sec...I think I know how to do it. I saw it in the movie *The Wizard of Oz*. You just click your ruby red slippers together and repeat: *There's no place like home...There's no place like home.*"

"But I don't want to go to Kansas! And I don't have any ruby red slippers. I have blue Reeboks."

"Perfect! They'll take you right to the dock on the shore of Lake Wichiganawaneehoohaw."

CHAPTER 3

Back at Camp Wichiganawaneehoohaw, Janet was roused from her flashbacks by the ringing of the lunch bell, accompanied by a woman's voice shouting, "Lunch Bell!"

"Oh," thought Janet, "That must be the lunch bell."

Janet rose quickly, then felt lightheaded and nearly lost her balance. The Northern Pike lurking below the dock eyed her with anticipation, hoping for a stumble into the lake leading to a feast of teenage girl fingers.

Suddenly, the voice of Karen Carpenter broke in: *And the only explanation I can find / Is the love that I've found ever since you've been around / Your love puts me on the top of the world.*

"Hello, daddy!" she said into her cell phone. "Calling to see how I'm doing?"

"Yeah," he said, "I just want to make sure my little pumpkin-eater isn't getting drunk and having sex with teenage boys."

"Daddy!" she screamed into the phone, "I'm trying to be friendly and you keep being mean! I'm not going to let you make me cry again. Besides, I think my tear glands are empty at the moment."

"Oh sure," he replied with disgust, "just as empty as my broken heart."

"That's the last straw, daddy!" she yelled. "Besides, what you just said makes no sense. I'm through with you! Good-*BYE!*"

And with that, she tossed the cell phone into the rippling blue waters of Lake Wichiganawaneehoohaw, where it was immediately swallowed by the Northern Pike.

Janet sauntered uneasily toward the main lodge. She would have sauntered easily, except that she didn't know what "sauntering" means.

Suddenly she felt a sharp pain in her neck, then heard the giggling of what sounded like a herd of munchkins. As she rubbed the sore spot on her neck, she pondered whether *herd* was the correct term for a gathering of munchkins.

A twig snapped behind her. She spun around, and from behind a bush popped a mop-topped fop.

"Haha!" laughed the fop in a Swedish accent. "My name is *Hjalmar*, da leader uf da Njördsöň Gang." Producing a straw, he added, "Howdja like getting shot wid my pea shooter? I gots good aim, ya?

"A pea shooter?" said Janet, rubbing her neck. "That's so 1950s! I suppose you also chew chlorophyll gum and hang out at the malt shop with Archie's gang, then put on a coonskin cap and do a panty raid on your way to watch The Mickey Mouse Club."

"Ooh!" said another popping fop, this one with less of a mop. "She's got lotsa spirit."

"Yeah," taunted the first sop. "For a *nerd!*"

"I am *not* a nerd!" said Janet. "Just because I read books and think about things like whether Darwin's theory of natural selection—although it can account quite well for 'microevolution' (variations within a given range of possibilities)—can account for macroevolution (the emergence of new ranges of possibility)."

"Nerd! Nerd!" shouted the second fop, who had neglected to introduce himself until this very moment. "My name's *Lars*, ya? I'm also a member of the Njördsöň Gang. My specialties are arson, theft, murder, and lying about my specialties."

"You better not mess with us!" said Hjalmar, "because ve are da coolest and toughest gang at Lake Wichiganawaneehoohaw Wayward Youth Recovery Camp."

"Oh, that's funny!" said Janet. "That's like saying you're the coolest and toughest gang in a place that isn't cool and tough at all."

"Ya!" said Hjalmar.

"Dot's right!" said the third and final fop, popping forth from the north. "Hjalmar know's wot he's talkin' about, ya?"

"Wow," said a surprised Janet, "your gang has girl members, too."

"I'm *Hulda*," said Hulda. "And I hof to say dot for a nerd youse ain't too smart."

"What are you talking about," asked Janet.

"Our gang can't have girl members," said Hulda.

"Why not?"

"Don't cha know that only *guys* have members?"

The three members of the Njördsöň Gang broke into riotous laughter as a humiliated Janet stormed off toward the main lodge.

Opening the door, she spotted a stout middle-aged woman with a bright red scarf tied around her silvery hair. "Uf da!" she announced to a crowd of rampaging kids. "Everybody git yerself down to a table, ya?"

She noticed Janet looking a bit disoriented, and came over to introduce herself.

"You must be da new girl, ya?" she said, holding out a ladle full of tater tot casserole. "My name is *Lena*. And you are...?"

Janet replied brightly, "Hi, I'm Janet, brightly," then shook Lena's ladle.

"Well, pleased ta meet ya, Janet Brightly," she said with a wide smile. "My name's still Lena. What do ya tink of da camp?"

"It's just what the brochure promised: Beautiful forests, fresh air, and lots of Swedish accents."

"Vot accents you talkin' about? Everybody here talks normal, ya?"

Rather than get into a ridiculous conversation, Janet asked, "Lena, how long have you been working here."

"Oh, me and hubby Ole, we's been runnin' dis camp for purt near thurty years now."

"Wow, thirty years! That's really—"

"Okay, enough chit chat! Time to eat! You just sit yerself down dere by doze hooligans and good-fer-nuttin's."

Hulda pointed her ladle to a large table full of thugs, drug burnouts, former prostitutes, future prostitutes, grungies, punks, crunks, thunks, and one smiling young blonde girl wearing a unicorn rainbow t-shirt.

"And dot table over dere?" she said, pointing her ladle to a smaller table, "Dot's our camp counselors und helper-outers."

Janet rubbed her eyes, thinking that she was seeing septuplets, a table full of identical blonde mop topped teens. "How can you tell them apart?" she asked.

"Why wouldja need to do dot?" answered Hulda. "All youse gots to remember is, da boy ones is called *Sven*, und da girl ones is called *Lena*."

Janet locked eyes with one of the Svens—and was stopped cold. It was *him*—the rude Swedish boy from the dock.

He was looking at her with disapproving eyes. *Husker Du, it's dot one from da lake!* he thought to himself with a Swedish accent.

After four large helpings of tater tot casserole followed by dessert of fruit-filled green Jell-O® topped with Cool Whip®, America's favorite brand of whipped topping, Janet was slowly crawling out of the dining room toward the door. On the way she was stopped by Lena.

"Hey Janet, "she asked. "How long hof ve known each other?"

"Oh, we chatted for about a minute I suppose."

"Well I yust vont you to know," said Lena in a wistful tone as her eyes got moist and the lighting got soft and atmospheric, "dot in all that time I've grown quite fond of you. In fact, I'm going to think of you as a 'surrogate daughter' from now on. I have a feeling that we'll bond yust like a real mother and daughter, yust like in da movies where dey do dat."

"Really?" said Janet, who eyes also got moist so they wouldn't fall behind. "That would be just great! Because my real mother...well, she...oh, it's so hard to explain."

Janet grew visibly upset. Her eyes got so moist that you could swear a tear was going to form. But not yet. Later there will be tears. Good lord, will there be tears. Just you wait.

"Oh, dot's all right, Janet," said a warm and reassuring Lena. "Later there will be tears. Now's not the time for our emotional bonding, not on a full stomach. Why don't cha c'mon over for tea tomorrow morning? We can have a nice chat. You can meet my hubby Ole. By any chance are you in the market for a surrogate father?"

"Oh, that's okay. I have a real father. Although our relationship isn't exactly...oh, it makes me want to cry!"

"Later!" said Lena. "Now you got to work off dot lunch so you can make room for dinner, ya?"

"I don't think I can eat for another week!" protested Janet.

"Dinner is in two hours!"

"Uf da!" said Janet, even though she wasn't Swedish.

Janet left the main lodge and headed toward her assigned cabin. Soon, she was crawling past a group of punk rockers that were cursing, spitting, spray-painting graffiti, manufacturing methamphetamines, setting fire to each other, and using bad grammar.

Janet gazed wistfully upon them. *I'll never be able to have such children*, she thought to herself, *to love and raise, then abandon once they turn bad. Not only that, but I'll never be able to do that thing that has to be done before a woman can have children. No man would want her! What man would want a woman who, at any time, might suddenly rip off his arm or try to eat his brains?*

"No," she said out loud to nobody in particular, "I have no future."

One of the punk rockers spray-painted *NO FUTURE* onto a tree.

Janet crawled slowly on, oblivious to everything but her own despair. She said out loud, again to nobody in particular but to a different nobody in particular, "All I can do is try to live for the moment."

A female voice answered, "You are so right! Because the present moment is all we have!"

Janet looked up to see the baldheaded van driver with the Mona Lisa smile. "It's like the Buddha taught," she said airily. "If you're focused on being somewhere else later on, then you can't be here now."

It was more than Janet could take. She collapsed and passed out. The punk rocker spray-painted on her back *NO CONSCIOUSNESS*.

CHAPTER 4

When Janet regained consciousness later that night, she found herself in a cabin lit by dozens of candles. The flames cast a warm orange glow upon the bald head of the van driver, who was meditating serenely in the center of a beautiful oriental rug. Janet looked around the cabin interior, noticing a string of Buddhist prayer flags hung from the rafters and a large poster of The Buddha with the words: IF YOU SEE THE BUDDHA ON THE HIGHWAY, TELL HIM TO HIT THE ROAD.

"What in heck does *that* mean?" asked Janet out loud.

"Oh, you're awake!" said the suddenly non-meditating van driver. "Actually, none of us are really *fully* awake, but that's what we're supposed to be working on, right? Oh—I never introduced myself. My name is *Aimee*. You're confused by my poster, huh?"

"Well, yes," said Janet. "I mean, if you're a Buddhist why wouldn't you want to see The Buddha?

I mean, Christians all want to see Christ. Aren't they all waiting for the Second Helping?"

"That's the Second *Coming*," corrected Aimee. Then she looked at the poster of the chubby smiling Buddha, and added, "But it sure looks like Buddha had a *second helping!*"

"Or maybe a *third!*" added Janet with a giggle.

The two women laughed and laughed, signifying that they had bonded.

But suddenly Aimee's face turned sad.

"What's wrong?" asked a concerned Janet.

"It's nothing," said Aimee, wiping away the beginnings of a tear.

"Aimee," said Janet, "now that we've instantly bonded into best friends forever, we have to tell each other *everything*."

"Everything?"

"Well, not about going to the bathroom and stuff like that," clarified Janet. "Everything *important*. And by 'important' I mean *deeply emotional and as dramatic as possible*."

"Okay, I will. I need to tell somebody. It's tearing me up inside. I'm so unhappy! I could just...I could just..."

"You could just die?" asked Janet.

"No, I could meditate and observe my feelings. But observing sad feelings just makes me feel sad."

A sliver of moonlight beamed through the cabin window, illuminating Aimee's face in a way that looked really dramatic and encouraged her to share her sad feelings.

"It's my boyfriend," Aimee continued, moonlight glistening on her bald head. "Back in Minneapolis. He's the reason I'm working up here this summer. I had to get away for a while."

"To escape from his physical and emotional abuse? To free yourself of his drug-filled gangster lifestyle?"

"No!" said Aimee. "Nothing like that!"

"To escape a life of prostitution?" asked an increasingly excited Janet. "Your boyfriend is your pimp? Are you also a heroin addict?"

"Hey Janet?" asked Aimee. "Has anyone ever told you that you might be a *drama addict?* It's nothing so crazy like that. I just need to sort out my feelings about him."

"That's not very interesting," said a disappointed Janet. "Not very dramatic at all."

"Drama is strictly avoided by Buddhists," explained Aimee. "Drama is based on the ego, which Buddhists hope to transcend. Drama is based on things like jealousy, greed, envy, lust—all which are based on reinforcing the illusion of the separate self."

As Janet began yawning and pretended to check the non-existent watch that wasn't on her arm, Aimee grew desperate to keep her attention.

"As for my boyfriend," Aimee added, "I think he might be a *zombie.*"

"REALLY?" said a re-energized and very interested Janet. "But why would you go out with a zombie?"

"Because I'm not sure! He's either an enlightened Buddhist Master, or a mindless zombie. Either he's achieved the ultimate state of "no-mind" or else he has no mind. "It's so hard to tell the difference!"

"Does he drool?"

"Well, a little. But I know many drooling Buddhists, so that's not a reliable sign."

"Does he feast on human brains?"

"Mostly beer and tortilla chips—while he's watching television. He likes football a lot. But zombies don't eat *only* brains, right? That wouldn't be a very balanced diet."

"I'm not sure!"

"Me either!" said Aimee. "That's why I'm here, to get some distance so I can sort out my feelings. Can I tell you a secret?"

"Ohmigod YES!" shouted Janet with glee. "But I'm not a drama addict."

"Okay, then. He's my first serious boyfriend. That's one reason it's so hard for me to tell if we have a dysfunctional relationship."

"Or if he's a zombie."

"I have nothing to compare to. I don't know what a 'normal' relationship is like with a non-zombie."

"Maybe you could find a sort of 'summer boyfriend' here at Lake Wichiganawaneehoohaw Wayward Youth Recovery Camp?"

"And not tell my boyfriend about it? Is that ethically okay?"

"Well," reasoned Janet, "if he's really an enlightened Buddhist Master he wouldn't be jealous, right? And if he's really a zombie he wouldn't be able to understand it."

"Hey, you're right!" said a pleased Aimee. "Cool! I've got lots of birth control with me. Do you know of any attractive and fairly hygienic guys that might like to go out with me?"

"Well, this morning I noticed that Nels was looking at your butt."

"Nels?" said Aimee. "I don't think I know a guy named Nels. Could you describe him to me?"

"He's really cute! You can recognize him from his tousled brown hair and his green eyes that will be looking at your butt."

"Okay," said Aimee. "I'll keep my eyes open! Thanks for helping me out!"

"Of course! Helping each other is my whole philosophy of life. I always say, *the only way to fulfil myself is by fulfilling others.*"

"You mean by touching them in their special place?"

"That's not what I mean at all!" protested Janet.

"If you say so," said Aimee. "Now it's your turn to tell me some deep emotional truth. Do you have religious beliefs?"

"Oh no, I'm a secular humanist. I've seen too many examples of people using religion not for love but for hatred and prejudice."

Janet's smiley face suddenly turned to a frowny face.

"Unfortunately," she sniffed, "one of those examples is *my own father!*"

Janet felt tears welling up.

"Oh no, girl!" shouted Aimee, "If you're gonna cry, grab a bucket. This rug cost me a fortune, although technically I'm supposed to be 'letting go' of material things like rugs."

"Well, maybe it's a good idea sometimes to let go of things. For example, *porcupines.*"

"Oh!" said Aimee, excitedly. "That's a great metaphor!"

"It wasn't a metaphor."

"Buddhism teaches us to be unattached," explained Lena, "because attachment is the root of sorrow."

Janet thought about that for a moment, then asked, "But what about *seat belts?* If you're in a car wreck I think staying attached to the seat would *prevent* sorrow."

"You're being too literal!" scolded Aimee. "I'd love to explain more, and share how Buddhism has changed my life. How much time to you have?"

"Time?" replied a wistful Janet, who began sobbing. "Oh…I suppose I have *the entire rest of my life!*"

"Hey!" yelled Aimee, "Use the bucket!"

CHAPTER 5

Next morning, Janet awoke—as she so often did in the morning. But for how many more mornings she did not know. It was obviously a somewhat sensitive subject, and not a good idea to ask unless you had access to a bucket.

Lena was asleep next to her, tightly clutching a stuffed Tony the Tiger™ doll. Janet quietly tip-toed outside and meandered toward Lena and Ole's cabin. She did much better at meandering that sauntering, since she knew exactly what meandering was. She was a poor saunterer but an okay meanderer.

As she approached the cabin, she noticed a peculiar aroma. She couldn't quite figure out what it was, but it reminded her of the air fresheners used in the bathrooms of fast food restaurants. As she lifted the door knocker and gave three solid knocks, she noticed a hand-painted sign on the wall that said, VELCOMMEN! and below that, *Dot means c'mon in!*

"Janet!" gushed Lena, opening the door. "My surrogate daughter! So good to see you!"

"Thanks, surrogate mother!" gushed Janet right back. Janet could gush with the best of them. And speaking of gushing... "Um, Lena? What's that aroma?"

"Oh, you mean da smell? Dot's the tea. It's a special ting called *pine needle tea*. It's an old recipe passed down from Grandma Tofte. The ingredients are hot water and pine needles."

"Oh, that's why it smelled like I was in a Burger King bathroom."

"Huh?"

"Never mind."

"Ya sure! Here's a nice cup of pine needle tea for you!"

"Um... thanks," said Janet, not gushing with enthusiasm this time. She took a sniff of the tea and her olfactory system shut down in self-defense.

"Hey Lena," she said, "Why is there a badger by the fireplace?"

"What?" shouted Lena, "Where is dot badger?"

As Lena looked hard to spot the non-existent badger, Janet dumped the tea into the pot of a houseplant which promptly turned brown and died.

"Well, dot's enough small talk, ya?" said Lena. "Let's get to our bonding!"

"Okay! So Lena, why have you become a surrogate mother to me?"

"Well, I needed a surrogate daughter to fill a void in my soul. You see, I had a daughter long ago. But she was... she was..."

"What?... What?..."

"Well it's... it's..."

"It's... it's what?"

"It's... it's hard to say."

"It sure is! Why are we having such trouble finishing a sentence?"

"Well, it tink you fixed it now, ya?"

"Ya! I mean, *yes!* So what were you saying about your daughter?"

"Oh Janet, it's so sad! She was killed by a zombie!"

"Oh no, Lena! I'm so sorry! Was she eaten by a zombie?"

"No, she was run over by a truck driven by a zombie."

"What a coincidence! My real mother was killed by a zombie."

"Eaten by a zombie?"

"No, she was crushed by a zombie that fell out of an airplane."

"Oh, I'm so sorry!" said Janet.

"Well, at least one good ting has come out of it. Dot is the reason me and Ole started Lake Wichiganawaneehoohaw Wayward Youth Recovery Camp. It's because we lost our own daughter before she could screw up her life and become a wayward youth like you."

"But it's not true!" protested Janet. "It was all a misunderstanding!"

"Dot's what dey all say," said Lena. "As I was saying, since we never had a chance to get rid of our own misbehaving child, we started dis camp for other misbehaving children that needed to be gotten rid of."

"That's noble, I suppose," said Janet. "But not a very positive view toward the concept of the nuclear family."

"Oh Janet," said Lena, "I love you as if you my own real daughter, wit da same unconditional love that every real mother feels for her real daughter. I'm so happy! Nothing could ever effect my love for you."

"Really? Nothing? Oh, I'm so happy!"

"Well, nothing except if youse was turning into a zombie like da one dot killed my real daughter."

"Oh no!" said a suddenly sad Janet, whose happiness was turning into upsetness. "I'm so... I'm so..."

"Oh, gosh durn it," said Lena, now youse da one dot got stuck. What's wrong?"

"It's nothing," said Janet while thinking of a lie. "I was just thinking about starving babies."

Just at that moment, or very close to that moment (let's not get too technical about it) Ole walked into the room, carrying a half-gallon jug of peppermint schnapps.

"Oh Ole, dere you is!" said Lena. "Sit down wit us and have some pine needle tea."

"Uf da!" said Ole. "Hey Lena, how come dere's a badger by the fireplace?"

"Not annuder one!" shouted Lena, searching once again for a thing which existed in no way in the earthly realm of tangible reality. Meanwhile, Ole dumped his tea into another doomed houseplant. As an aside which contributes nothing to this story and very possibly detracts from it, Lena spent much of her life pondering why so many of her houseplants died while having guests over for tea.

Ole gave Janet a "wink" which signified they had bonded over their mutual success in screwing up Lena's thought process.

"The only way I can drink dot stuff is with a little *spice*," he announced, while filling the cup with peppermint schnapps.

"Hey Ole," said Lena. "D'ya remember when you proposed marriage?"

"Oh, ya! I told you dot if you married me I would either churn you ten pounds of butter or write you a poem."

"Ya! So I married you for butter or verse!"

"Ya, you sure did, Lena! And d'ya remember dot for our honeymoon ve vere driving down to Lutsen, on the north shore of Lake Superior?"

"Ya! And while you were driving you put your hand on my knee. Then I said, real flirty, 'Oh Ole, you can go a little farther if you vant to."

"So I drove us to Duluth."

"But Ole, you remember in Duluth how you had some trouble with da police?"

"Oh, dot's right, Lena! The police officer pulled me over and told me I was doing 50 in a 30 zone. I told him, 'No officer, I'm sure I vas doing only 30.'"

"And he was very insistent, ya? 'No, you were doing 50,' he said."

"And I told him right back, 'Really officer, I vas only doing 30.' And he said back, 'But I clocked you doing 50.'"

"So I tried to help out. I told him, 'Officer you really shouldn't argue with Ole ven he's been drinking.' Uf-da, it vas so funny!"

"Vel, maybe more funny for you den for me, ya?"

"Hey Ole, it vas no picnic for me either, spendin' our honeymoon watchin' da television in a Motel 6 while you was in da drunk tank."

"Oh Lena," said Ole. "we's bein' rude to our young guest here. She's probably not interested in hearin' boring stories from a couple of old farts. By the way, who is she?"

"Ole, this is Janet," said Lena. "She's our surrogate daughter."

"Pleased to meet you, Ole," said Janet. "I have a real dad, so you don't have to remember my name. But since he's not here and we're currently estranged from each other, you can be my *temporary* surrogate father. Hey, wasn't it fun when we took turns screwing up Lena's thought process?"

"Well," pondered Ole, "I suppose I can love you like a real daughter. As long as you don't—"

"Turn into a zombie?" asked Janet.

"No," answered Ole. "As long as you don't fall for that *Sven* character who works here. He's a bad apple if ever I saw one, and also a bad rutabaga. And pretty much a bad version of any fruit or vegetable I can tink of. He's a hopeless womanizer. He just loves 'em and leaves 'em. Actually, I don't tink he even loves 'em. He just leaves 'em—after he's done makin' da whoopee. So I absolutely, positively forbid you from falling for him."

"Thanks, Ole!" said Janet. "But are you aware that by forbidding an inappropriate teen relationship you're basically guaranteeing that it will happen?"

"Vot's your name again?" asked Ole. "And why are you usin' such big words?"

CHAPTER 6

It was the next morning, and Janet had walked to the shore of the lake. The sun was just coming up. Or actually—as Janet's scientific mind was well aware—the revolving earth had once again reached the point where the spot occupied by Janet was perpendicular to the rays of the local star that we call the *sun*: the immense source of gravitational attraction keeping all the planets in the solar system spinning in an orderly fashion and not just freaking out all over.

And while the expression "What a nice sunrise!" was not scientifically accurate, it sounded a lot nicer than "What a nice rotational star-greeting perpendicularity."

A fine mist played upon the surface of the lake, dancing a slow swirl to subtle breezes. Suddenly the muffled voice of what sounded like Karen Carpenter emerged from the lake: *Something in the wind has learned my name / And it's telling me that things are not the same.*

Then a small part of the lake began frothing and churning, and out of the bubbling violence leapt an immense and pissed-off Northern Pike. *How can I get a decent night's sleep,* thought the Northern Pike, *with that damn thing going off every twenty minutes?*

As shocked as Janet was, she was even more shocked to hear the muffled voice of her father emerging from the water: "Janet, this is your father...again! Please pick up. Do you know where the keys to the shed are? Also, I miss you."

She realized what must have happened: The Northern Pike had swallowed her cell phone!

Janet had barely recovered from the shock, when suddenly a loud voice boomed from behind her: "UF-DA! DOT WAS SHURE A PURDY SUNRISE, YA?"

"Sven!" she yelled, her heart racing, "What are you trying to do, give me a heart attack?"

"I don't tink you'll believe me," said Sven, "but I coulda swore dot fish was singin' to me. Crazy, ya? Nuttin' like dot woulda happened in da 80s."

"The 80s!" gushed Janet. "Okay, you've *got* to know this one: *Strut on a line, discord and rhyme / I'm on the hunt I'm after you / Mouth is alive, juices like wine / and I'm hungry like the wolf.*"

"Huh?" he said. "If youse is hungry dey be serving breakfast in a little while, ya?"

"What?" replied a shocked Janet. "There's *no way* you can not know that one!"

Alone with Sven, she felt strange. She was pleased to see him yet also loathed everything about him. She didn't know whether to give him a hug or smash him with a tire iron. This made no sense to her, unless it meant that they were destined to become emotionally involved.

"Well, in case ya want to do some fishin' dis morning," said Sven, "I would be glad to bait your hook."

Janet was confused. Why was Sven suddenly being so nice to her?

Against her better judgment, Janet was shocked to hear herself reply, "Oh yes, I love fishing," when she had never fished in her life. Growing up in St. George, she had only seen photographs of fishing.

Sven was confused. Why was he suddenly being so nice to Janet? *I haf had my heart broke by dese kinda city-slicker girls*, he thought to himself. *But sometin tells me dis Janet is maybe not like da udders.*

He was suspicious of Janet's intelligence, due to a tragic aspect of his childhood. In school he admired the smart kids, but that admiration was not reciprocated. Not even a little. He was relentlessly teased by the smarter kids, which were all the other kids.

He sensed that Janet was trouble. She obviously had smarts in her brains. He thought back to the previous summer, when he'd fallen for a smart girl that had toyed with his affection. She tried to make him understand Immanuel Kant's *categorical imperative* and Sven thought it was a recipe for fried catfish. He'd learned from that experience to be wary of girls that weren't as dense as dirt.

Just then, the members of the Njördsön Gang ambled nearby. It was a purposeful amble—an amble with spunk and attitude. Not a lazy amble which could be confused with sauntering or meandering.

They hadn't quite spotted Sven. He was about to yell something at them, some tough gang-talk. In the Njördsön Gang, as in all tough and cool gangs, insults are considered terms of endearment. For example, in tough New Jersey gangs, telling a fellow gang member "I like you better dead" means "Good morning!" In Minnesota, the situation was somewhat less extreme.

Sven was working up some good options. Perhaps he would yell at them, "Hey, worm lickers!" or "None of you can't catch fish fer nuttin'!"

But just as he was about to shout, he had a realization in his mind. This was not a familiar sensation for Sven. The last time it happened was... Actually, it had never happened. His realization was: *The Njördsön Gang is the coolest and toughest gang at Lake Wichiganawaneehoohaw Wayward Youth Recovery Camp. If they see me talking to a smarty-pants city-slicker like Janet, then...*

And in less than two Swedish heartbeats, Sven was hiding behind a tree, waiting for the Njördsön Gang to continue ambling right on by.

If Sven had read books about psychology and was able to understand what he'd read, he would have recognized the feeling as *cognitive dissonance*. He had two incompatible feelings: One—He wished to remain in good standing with The Njördsön Gang and retain valuable "street cred" even though all the streets at Lake Wichiganawaneehoohaw Wayward Youth Recovery Camp were dirt roads. Two—He found himself curiously not-hating Janet. But he knew that if he was seen with her publicly he would be branded "un-cool."

Just then, the gang noticed Janet standing there suddenly alone, wondering where Sven had suddenly vanished to.

"Nerd alert!" shouted one of them, possibly Hjalmar. No wait, it was Lars. Honestly, it's really hard to tell them apart.

Then Lars (I'm positive) yelled, "Ya! What he said!" followed by Hulda who yelled, "I can't really add anyting new to what dey said!"

After the gang had ambled out of view, probably to harass squirrels, Sven cautiously came out from behind the tree.

"What's wrong, Sven?" said Janet. "You're not ashamed to be seen with me, are you?"

"Oh no, dot's not it at all."

"You're not experiencing *cognitive dissonance* due to your conflicted feelings, are you?"

"Oh no! Dot can't be it because I don't know what you just said."

"Okay," said Janet, "I'll just naively believe you due to my innocent and trusting nature."

"No, dot's not it either."

"Huh?" said an appropriately confused Janet, shaking her head to rid her brain of muddled thoughts. "Let's change the subject. Do you like fishing."

"Oh ya!" said Sven, brightening up with interest. "Fishing is my favorite ting! Fishing is my life! You're interested in fishing, ya?"

"No."

"Okay, den. I tell ya all about it!" He opened his prize tackle box, which had suddenly appeared out of nowhere. He showed Janet the top tray, which was divided into separate compartments. "Dis is where I keep all my lures. Usin' da right lure is da most important part of fishing."

"Lures? What do they do?"

"The lure is vot you cast out into da water. Each one is designed to be somethin' that a certain kind of fish wants to eat at a certain time of da year. You can buy lures, but true fishermen make the lures themselves by hand."

"Is that because your careful study of the dietary habits of fish and the surrounding habitat gives you a better idea of how to design the lure to fit the ecosystem?"

"No, because it's cheaper. Now, here's one of my favorite lures. It's called the *wooly worm*."

"What kind of fish is it designed to catch?" asked Janet.

"Fishes dot like wooly worms. Janet, for such a smart girl you really ain't too smart."

"Well, maybe not about fishing, but I'm very well-educated when it comes to plate tectonics and subduction zones."

"Are dose kinds of lures?"

"Not exactly," said Janet. "They're geological processes that have created the physical landscape on which we play out our earthly existence, living and learning and growing as we go."

"So anyway," continued Sven, producing the next lure. "Dis one is called *roast beef sandwich*."

"Wow, the workmanship is amazing," said Janet, examining the lure which looked exactly like a roast beef sandwich. "How did you find the materials to exactly duplicate the look and texture of a roast beef sandwich?"

"It was easy," said Sven. "I went to Lena in the kitchen and said, 'Hey Lena, make me a roast beef sandwich.' Okay, dis next one I call *teenager finger*. Dis one works real good at Lake Wichiganawa-neehoohaw. Da fish here is eatin' teenager fingers all da time. Do ya want to touch it? It's very realistic."

"Eww!" said Janet, backing away from the very realistic dead finger with a fishing hook coming out of the fingernail. "I don't want to know where you found the materials for this one! Can you show me how you catch one? Can you catch a fish for me right now?"

"Ya shure!" said Sven. "Catchin' fish is purdy easy for me, I yust cast out the lure like dis..."

Sven cast out the lure like dat, and it sailed far out into the blue wetness of Lake Wichiganawaneehoohaw. But before the lure even touched the water, a large trout leapt into the air, grabbed the lure with its fin, hooked itself in the lower lip, and swam quickly back to shore where it crawled up to Sven. It stood upright on its tail fin and looked up to him, opening its gills with an expression of submissive expectation.

"...and dot's how I catches da fish," continued Sven, lifting the trout by its gills in a male's typically misguided effort to impress a female.

"Wow," said Janet, "that's really impressive!"

Apparently in this case the effort was not at all misguided. You can never tell with people.

"But I had lotsa practice, ya?"

"You make it look so easy," she beamed, suddenly very proud of Sven. Not that he was her boyfriend or anything. All she knew is that Sven suddenly looked pretty good right at that moment, standing there with his big ten-inch trout.

"Now it's your turn!" said Sven.

"M-m-me?" stammered Janet, who so rarely stammered that nobody suspected she was a stammerer. "But I've never fished before in my life. I've only seen photographs of fishing."

Producing a fishing rod, Sven said, "Here ya go!" and placed the rod in her tender pink hands, gently wrapping her delicate pink fingers around the thick handle.

"Uf-da!" he complained. "I tink it gittin kinda warm out here, ya?"

"Oh, that must be the steadily increasing solar energy," answered Janet, "caused by the earth's rotational star-greeting perpendicularity."

"Ya!" said Sven. "And also because da sun is gettin' higher up."

"Show me how to catch a Northern Pike," requested Janet, "For example, a Northern Pike that has a cell phone in its stomach."

"Well, dis it what ya gotta do," he said, guiding one of her lovely slender virgin fingers to the reel lock. "Ya put yer finger here on da trigger, ya? Und den you hold onto dis rod as hard as you can. Und den, ven da rod starts throbbing, you know dot you got yurself a big one."

Janet felt lightheaded and woozy at the touch of Sven's strong hands. She felt a strange feeling she'd only felt once before, while watching Johnny Depp in the movie *Cry-Baby*.

Janet suddenly bolted upright. "I—I can't do this!" she stammered. "I don't even *like* fish! I'm—I'm a *vegetarian!*"

She dropped the fishing rod and bolted away.

"Vot's wrong?" said a confused Sven, "Ve vere hoffing such a gute time!"

Just then the breakfast bell rang, followed by Lena shouting, Breakfast Bell!" Janet ran toward the lodge, tears welling up in her confused seventeen-year-old eyes. Would she be able to sort out all these strange and baffling feelings before she turned into a...? But maybe she wouldn't turn into a...? Suddenly Janet felt a ray of hope, and she felt something like a smile form on her lips.

The breakfast bell rang again, and she suddenly realized how hungry she was. She craved a good hearty meal. *Of human flesh!*

"Oh *no!*" she sobbed, immense tear blobs splashing on the ground.

CHAPTER 7

Having a bit of food in her stomach helped to settle Janet's turbulent emotions. Breakfast was a hearty stack of buckwheat pancakes, a steaming plate of hash browns smothered in mushroom gravy, a four-egg omelet, a dozen links of TVP®-based vegetarian sausage, a toasted loaf of bread, and a fruit cup.

Yes, Janet was definitely more grounded and "down to earth," bounded by the extra gravitational pull of 30 pounds of food in her stomach.

She felt her protruding belly and thought to herself, *Well, at least I know what it's like to be pregnant.*

Eventually, Janet was able to drag herself upright and slowly shuffle outside to the front deck of the lodge. She considered descending the stairs, but decided it was too risky because of the possibility of falling. If she fell in her current condition, she reasoned, she would pop. She decided to rest on the big porch swing rather than risk being remembered as "that girl who popped."

She gazed upon the deep blue waters of Lake Wichiganawaneehoohaw, and once again she was mesmerized by the calming ripples. She suddenly had the urge to make a wish. *Oh rippling blue water*, she thought to herself. *I know this is extremely irrational and goes against everything I believe in, but just in case everything I believe is wrong can you grant me one tiny wish?*

The rippling blue water continued rippling.

Okay, thought Janet, *I didn't hear a 'no' so I'll interpret that as a 'yes.'*

The ripples in the blue water got bigger, as if to say, "Oh Janet, tell me your wish before my ripples turn into large crashing waves and crush all the nice canoes lined up on the beach!"

Okay, Okay! thought Janet. *Just settle down and I'll tell you.*

The rippling water settled down, but it was just a coincidence. It was planning on settling down anyway.

First of all, thought Janet, *I wish for peace on earth and all that so I don't sound selfish. Secondly, please stop these feelings I have for Sven...the Sven that uses language that sounds like it was from an old man...the one with the big, strong Swedish hands...the hands that feel so good on my delicate young virgin teenage fingers.*

A gust of wind created a violent swath of rippling upon the blue water.

Oh, you're right, continued Janet. *Maybe I'm getting a little emotionally involved. But that's the problem! I can't allow it! He doesn't know my secret. I couldn't do that to him! I couldn't put him through that!*

The ripples in the rippling blue water became slow and sensuous.

No! thought Janet. *I am not horny! Just who do you think are, rippling blue water? Just because you're blue and rippling and happen to be right, you think you're so smart. Oh, sacred rippling blue water, I hereby make a sacred vow to have nothing to do with Sven. I shall avoid him like the plague. I don't even like him! In fact, I hate him! I absolutely and utterly loathe everything about him!*

"Oh *here* you are," said Sven. "Vant to go fer a valk?"

"Oh, I'd *love* to!" gushed Janet.

Hey! thought the rippling blue water. *What about that 'sacred vow'?*

"Do we have to go for a 'valk'?" asked Janet, totally ignoring the rippling blue water now that a handsome guy showed up.

"Huh?"

"I mean, I don't know how to walk in Swedish. How about if we take a *stroll* instead?"

"A *stroll*?"

"Oh good! We pronounce it the same! Let's take a stroll by the lake."

As they strolled along the shore of the wet water, amidst the towering woody things sticking up all over the place, they felt no need to talk. Janet did not speak because she was overwhelmed with the natural beauty. Sven did not speak because Janet didn't ask him any questions about fishing. Since strolling silently amidst natural beauty makes for a very dull story, Janet finally spoke up.

"Sven, I'm surprised that you asked me to go on a valk."

"Well," said Sven, "if youse fishing for walleye in the early spring it's no good usin' lures."

"Huh?"

"Dose walleye ain't used to seein' flies and udder bugs until June, so dey don't bite. You do better by usin' live bait."

"Sven, I have a feeling you're using all this talk about fishing to hide your real feelings."

"Worms work purdy good, but minnows is better if you can find 'em."

"Sven, be honest with me," said Janet. "Do you like me?"

"Oh, I suppose I don't mind you hangin' around," said Sven, smiling and looking at Janet with his piercing blue eyes.

"I think it's amazing how well we get along," she said, gazing thoughtfully upon the lake, "seeing as how we are such two different people." After more thoughtful gazing upon the lake, she added: "But in stories like this it's very important that the main characters be opposites."

"You mean... like I'm da 'bad boy' and youse is the 'goody-two-shoes'?"

"Yes!"

"And you came from a sheltered background, ya?"

"It's true! I did!"

"And you're all innocent of the ways of life dot I know all about."

"It's the kind of contrast William Blake wrote about in his poems *Songs of Innocence* and *Songs of Experience*."

"If you say so," said Sven. "I was thinkin' more about how you don't understand what it means that I'm the camp stud who all da' women wanna bone."

"Huh?"

"Dot's exactly what I mean!"

"Well," said Janet, "I was thinking more along the lines of how I'm very smart, but you have an intelligence quotient incapable of comprehending complex sentences with large words, like this one I'm saying right now."

"Huh?"

"Exactly! Oh, Sven! I feel as if we're overcoming differences and growing as individuals. We might even be getting emotionally involved, but I'm not sure. I'm innocent of the ways of life that you know all about. For example, this might be the appropriate time for a hug. What do you think?"

"Well, I was tinking dot it was time for our clothes to come off."

Just at that moment, like clockwork, The Njördsön Gang showed up before any clothes could come off. Due to the visual obfuscation of a maple sapling, they did not immediately see Janet.

"Hi Sven!" said Lars. "Good morning!"

"Lars!" scolded Hjalmar. "Dot's too friendly! We's the coolest and toughest gang at Lake Wichiganawaneehoohaw Wayward Youth Recovery Camp, ya?"

"Oh ya!" remembered Lars. "Okey-dokey I try startin' all over. Hey Sven, suck my trout!"

"Dot's better!" exclaimed Hjalmar.

"Hey, I gots a good one!" said Hulda. "Hey Sven, eat my head cheese!"

[Editor's Note: "head cheese" is a thoroughly disgusting concoction, unique to Scandinavian strongholds such as small towns in rural Minnesota and Wisconsin. It is not "cheese" in any sense of the term. It is a gelatinous mass holding together meat by-products. It is primarily made from—wait for it—parts of animal heads.]

"Ooh!" exclaimed Hjalmar. "Dot's a good one! I don't know if I gots a topper for dot one. How about: Hey Sven, I tink I saw youse hangin' out wit a—"

At that moment, from around the maple sapling, there appeared the youthful face of...

"—a *nerd?*"

Suddenly the entire membership of the coolest and toughest gang at Lake Wichiganawaneehoohaw Wayward Youth Recovery Camp saw their friend Sven.

Together.

With.

A nerd.

The thoughts within Sven's mind slowed down, even slower than usual. If before he had been able to obfuscate his cognitive dissonance by hiding behind a tree, now he could obfuscate no longer. He had a fundamental choice to make. He could admit that he liked Janet. Or at least that he didn't mind her hangin' around. He could exhibit courage, be a man, stand up for his beliefs. He could preserve the dignity of Janet, a young woman for whom he was beginning to have what some people call "feelings." Or he could...

"Oh, we're not hangin' out or nuttin like dot," said the cowardly Sven. "In fact, I was tinking about pushing her in da lake."

Janet was shocked into uncomprehending silence, staring at Sven in disbelief.

"Really!" said Hjalmar. "Why don't cha then?"

"I decided," said Sven who was getting more cowardly by the second, "dot she's not worth da trouble."

"Haha!" laughed Hulda. "A nerd ain't worth the trouble."

"Yeah!" agreed Lars. "And what if a snapping turtle ate a piece of her? It would probably poison the poor turtle!"

"Haha!" laughed Sven who could not possible get any more cowardly. "Hey, why don't we all play a game of ping-pong back at the recreation center, ya? You all go ahead, I'll meet you there."

"Why can't you come with us now?" asked Hulda.

"I have to tie my shoes," said Sven. "See you in half an hour."

"Okay!" said Hjalmar. "See you there."

And with that, The Njördsön Gang left, in a very cool and tough manner, saying rude things to every chipmunk and blue jay they encountered.

"Sven!" shouted a very upset and angry Janet. "How could you do such a thing to me? I thought you liked me?"

"Uf da! I didn't mean what I said to da gang! I was just—you know—*acting*. Just pretending, ya? I didn't mean none of dose words I said."

"To repeat my previous question that you haven't really answered: How could you do such a thing to me? I thought you liked me?"

"But Janet, I had to do it or else they make fun of me, ya?"

"Oh," she said as sarcastically as possible. "And that's such a terrible thing! To be made fun of by a bunch of munchkins! I thought we were friends!"

"Whoa! Is we friends?"

"Apparently," said Janet, even more sarcastically than last time, "Some people don't know *how* to be friends!"

"How 'bout we be secret friends?"

"*Secret* friends?"

"Ya! Friends only when nobody is looking at us, ya? But when dey be lookin' then we pretend we're not friends. That can work just fine, ya?"

If there would have been a door right there, you can be sure that Janet would have slammed it and stomped off to walk along a rain-soaked urban street at night. But it was daytime and there were no doors and her stomping didn't work very well in the beautiful green moss that carpeted the forest floor.

CHAPTER 8

The next morning it got light. It's a familiar story. You've heard it before, and you'll hear it again. But this morning was different. At least it was for one intelligent young woman whose tender heart had been broken. Metaphorically speaking, of course, because if her actual heart was broken she'd be dead.

She was sitting in the main lodge dining room, pondering the plate in front of her, wondering how 20 pounds of food was supposed to fit inside her 90-pound body. Far on the other end of the room was The Njördsöň Gang. Janet chose her seat specifically to be as far as possible from the annoying little freaks.

Then... *he* walked in (Sven, of course) looking unusually pensive, even though he probably doesn't know what the word *pensive* means. He headed toward the last open seat. Can you guess where the last open seat was? You're right if you guessed that it was right next to...

"Janet," said Sven. "Um... how 'bout I say 'Good Morning,' ya?"

"Oh, it's *you*," said Janet in such a cold tone that it triggered a snowstorm at the next table. "You should probably know that I'm not talking to you."

"Actually," said Sven, "you *are* talking to me. The words are coming out of your mouth."

"Oh," said Janet, observing her mouth reflected in the back of her spoon. "You're totally right."

"Mind if I sit in the last open seat that's next to you?"

"Really? But then people could see. I wouldn't want you to lose your reputation by talking to a *nerd*."

"Well," he said quietly, "maybe I don' care too much 'bout dot."

"Really?" she asked, beginning to warm up, beginning to think that maybe Sven had grown as an individual.

"Sven, why do you look so pensive?"

"Huh? What does that mean?"

[Editor's Note: We thought so!]

"Well, you can sit with me," said Janet, "as long as you promise me one thing."

"Ya sure, whatever."

"That you don't fall in love with me."

"Huh? Oh, I don't tink dot be a problem!"

"What?"

"I mean, I just tot you'd be good for da making whoopee, ya?"

"You're joking, right?"

"Um, I tink da answer I should say is 'yes,' ya?"

"Ya—I mean *yes*, I tink so. I mean, I *think* so. Gosh darn it! See how you're effecting me?"

"Is dis what you mean by growin' as individuals?"

"Um, not exactly. But if you're willing to be seen sitting with me, it means you've found courage. Or you're courage has grown wings and begun to fly. Or your courage has come out of the closet. I'm still working on a good metaphor. Because as soon as The Njördsön Gang sees you here with me, they'll start calling you a—"

"Nerd lover!" shouted Hjalmar!

"Sven has gone to the nerd side!" shouted Lars.

"You are officially no longer cool!" shouted Hulda. "None of da udder girls be making da whoopee with you now!"

"As leader of The Njördsön Gang," declared Hjalmar, "we are gonna stomp out of here and make a plan for a really mean prank for later in the story."

And they did exactly that, with their stomping sounding much better on the hardwood floor of the lodge than on the ground of the soft mossy forest.

"Gosh," said Janet, glowing with newfound respect or something. "You gave up all those other girls for me?"

"Um..." was all that Sven could muster, as his face grew pale.

"I think I know what's going on," she said.

"..." continued Sven, still stunned by the prospect of no more whoopee.

"You're scared."

"..." continued Sven, still stunned.

"You're scared that nobody would ever want to be with you in a *real* way, in a *genuine* way."

"I gave up all da whoopee for you?"

"And I respect you so much for it, you can't believe! Sven, this makes me respect you so much, I'm going to ask you something very special."

"Makin' da whoopee?"

"Oh Sven, you are so funny!"

"But I vasn't joking."

"I was going to ask you to go for a walk! Oh Sven, walk with me!"

"Well," reasoned Sven, "I suppose if dere's no whoopee we might was well walk, ya?"

"Maybe we can even hold hands?"

"Is dot a kind of foreplay?"

"Oh Sven, you make me laugh!"

"But I vasn't joking."

Off they went into the forest, which to Janet was suddenly the most beautiful place in the world. Everything was wonderful. She was happier than she'd ever been in her life. She was so happy that for the first time in days she'd totally forgotten about...*you know*.

Just then, a white-tailed deer ambled by peacefully.

"Aw, wouldja look at dot!" said Sven. "It's Bambi's mother!"

Suddenly, some strange feeling came over Janet. She began shaking, then drool formed on her lips. In a guttural roar, she shouted, "Brains! Must have brains!" then ran straight for the deer, shouting "Brains!" and making savage clawing motions with her hands.

"Janet! No!" yelled Sven. "It's not huntin' season for anoder month!"

But it was no use. Janet pounced upon the deer, which was *not* Bambi's mother. What was Sven thinking? Everyone who has seen the movie *Bambi* knows that Bambi's mother gets shot by a hunter. It's really unforgettable. How could anybody see the movie and forget that? Sorry for the spoiler if you haven't seen the movie yet.

"Must have brains!" cried Janet, trying to claw at the deer's head, but just sort of petting it a little too hard, which annoyed the deer.

"Stop!" cried Sven. "If dey catch you annoying a deer out of season, dey can trow you in jail!"

He grabbed her arm, trying to pull her off of what he thought was Bambi's mother. But it didn't work. And the deer was looking *really* annoyed. So he yanked hard on Janet's arm, which came off.

"Uf da! Sorry 'bout dot!"

Janet snapped back to her senses, and screamed out, "Oh no! It's still happening! I can't stop it!"

"Hey, dis is vierd," said Sven, examining the arm. "Why is dere no blood?"

"Give me my arm!" snapped Janet, snatching the arm with her other arm. "I suppose you think this is all kind of weird, huh?"

"Oh, no problem!" said Sven, matter-of-factly. "I see people's arms comin' off all da time."

"Oh, really?" said Janet, smiling.

"No, not really," said Sven, not smiling. "I just told you dot cause I tot it make you feel better if I say dot, ya?"

"No!" cried Janet, suddenly upset. "Not ya! Not ya!" she screamed, running toward the lodge. "I want to die! I wish I'd never been born!"

Actually, she thought to herself, slowing to a walk, *I'm fine with being born. But I wish that the weird boy who bit me at the party had never been born*.

Sven thought to himself, *I tink she's upset for some reason*, and watched her go back inside her cabin. He turned to gaze upon the waters of Lake Wichiganawaneehoohaw, which were still blue, but hardly rippling at all. All grew quiet.

Then a muted sound emerged from the blue and hardly-rippling-at-all waters: *In the leaves on the trees and the touch of the breeze / There's a pleasing sense of happiness for me.*

The water began to stir, then he heard the same muffled voice as before: "Janet, this is your father again…for the last time! Since you refuse to answer, you have left me with no choice but to come over and check on you in person. I'll be there next week. Please try to not get drunk or get pregnant until then. Also, I still haven't found the keys to the shed."

After the voice stopped, all was quiet except for what sounded like a Northern Pike ramming its head into the dock.

Suddenly, Sven felt a sharp pain in the neck.

"Ow!" he said, rubbing the sore spot.

As we all know, being shot with a pea shooter is one of the many ways guys show their affection for each other. Other ways include: verbal insults, slaps on the back, weird handshake routines that nobody else knows, and helping to fix their broken fishing reel. Otherwise, they might be forced to express "feelings." Possibly involving the use of "words."

Without even turning around, Sven said, "Hey dere Hjamlar. I see your aim is still gud. But why are you here talkin' to me? I tot da Njördsön Gang rejected me?"

"Best pea shooter in Lake Wichiganawaneehoohaw Wayward Youth Recovery Camp," said Hjalmar, beaming with pride and obviously not realizing how utterly non-impressive this statement was. "I'm not here as a member of the Njördsön Gang. I'm here as yer oldest and best friend. I just came by to express some feelings."

"Huh?"

"Using words."

"Oh no you don't! Dot's not how guys do tings!"

"It's okay," reassured Hjalmar. "I'll also help you fix your broken fishing reel."

"Well..." reasoned Sven, "I guess dot be okay. But don't cha know, I don't have dot broken fishing reel with me. It's back in my cabin, ya?"

"Dot's okay, we can just pretend to be fixin' it, ya?"

"Well, dot sounds much more easy than goin' all the way back to my cabin."

"Ya, dot would mean us having to move."

"Okay den," said Sven, "hand me da pretend pliers, will'ya?"

"Okey-dokey here you go," said Hjalmar, pretending to hand Sven a pliers, "but be careful, ya? The grip is loose and sometimes it slips off."

"Tanks for da warning! Okay, I got the cover off da pretend reel, I tink the problem might be dis lever here is stuck. Maybe I can get it loose wit da pliers."

"Careful, Sven."

"Hey don't tell me how to—*Ouch!*"

"What happened, Sven?"

"The stupid grip came off. I tore off the end of my thumb."

"Your real thumb?"

"No, da pretend thumb."

"Well Sven, while you pretend to put a band-aid on your thumb, I yust wanted to say I'm worried about you. Ever since you met this Janet...I don't know. She's changed you."

"Wot do you mean?" said Sven defensively.

"It's like you're not so mean as before. You don't go pea shooting with The Njördsöň Gang no more. We ain't harassed any of the new kids in almost a week. When's the last time we threw a kid into the lake or set them on fire?"

"It's weird, Hjalmar," said Sven, pretending to litter the forest by tossing away the pretend band-aid wrapper, "but dose kinda tings just don't sound like fun no more."

"It's because of dot Janet!"

"No!" protested Sven. "Yust because it happened at exactly the first time I saw her, dot has nothing to do with it!"

He then realized that pretending to litter the forest was not a very nice thing to do, so he picked up the pretend band-aid wrapper and placed it in his pocket, to pretend to throw into an approved trash receptacle later on.

"What'cha doin'?" cried Hjalmar. "Is youse crazy?"

"Vell, I yust realized dot dis forest here is kinda nice, so why spoil it with pretend litter? Pretend band-aid wrappers ain't biodegradable, and they have a negative effect on the local ecology."

"Sven! She *is* changing you! You never used to talk like dot! Next thing you know, she's going to have you reading a *book!*"

"A book?"

"Ya! It's a ting with pages dot got words on it."

"Is a book a bad ting?"

"Ya!" said Hjalmar, coming close to having a feeling. "It turns you into a *nerd!*"

"Well, if she ever tries to give me one of dose tings," said Sven, "I'll throw it into an approved trash receptacle. And she won't be my friend no more, ever again."

"I don't know Sven, I'm worried about you," said a worried-about-Sven Hjalmar. "If The Njördsöň Gang doesn't get the old Sven back, we might have to go through with our plan to do a really mean prank later in the story."

Just then, Ole walked by.

"Hello dere, Ole!" said Sven.

"Oh, hello dere Sven. I'm against you bein' friends wit Janet, my temporary surrogate daughter."

As Ole walked away, Sven wondered: Why was everybody against him being with Janet? He was starting to feel like a character in a dying teenage girl story.

CHAPTER 9

In the office of the lodge, Janet was sitting on the couch with Lena.

"Let me haf a look at dot arm," said Lena, who served the role of camp nurse in addition to serving ladles of casserole.

"Sure, here you go," replied Janet, handing her the arm.

"Does it hurt?"

"I have no idea, since it's not attached," said Janet, then added ironically, "Why don't you ask the arm?"

Having no sense of irony (typical of Swedes) Lena asked the arm, "So arm, does it hurt?" The arm did not reply, so she returned her attention to Janet. "You know, dot Sven he took it badly, eh? He tinks dis was all his fault. He felt so bad, he almost skipped lunch."

"Oh, that's silly!" said Janet. "It's just that when the arm came off he happened to be holding it, pulling as hard as he could."

"Well, I tink you bedder haf a talk wid him,"

Poor Sven, thought Janet. He did pull off her arm, but only to save the deer. Even though it wasn't Bambi's mother, it was still a nice gesture. Maybe this Sven really was okey-dokey?

"Lena?" asked Janet. "Do you think Sven likes me?" Then added, hopefully, "Even a little bit?" Then more hopefully, "Or maybe even a lot?"

"Vell," said Lena thoughtfully, "Did he ever say dot he likes you?"

"Well," said Janet, also thoughtfully, "He did say, 'I suppose I don't mind you hangin' around.'"

"Oh Janet!" exclaimed Lena. "He loves you!"

"What? Huh?"

"Swedes ain't very good at expressin' emotion, ya? My hubby Ole, the closest he ever came to talkin' about love was one time he told me, 'Lena, I suppose you can do the opposite of going away from me.' Janet, *I suppose I don't mind you hangin' around* is the most romantic expression of love possible for a Swede."

"Oh no!" said Janet, her eyes getting wet with pre-tears.

"Huh?" said Lena, "I tot you wanted him to like you lots?"

"Oh, Lena!" explained Janet. "My emotions are so mixed up! The tears that I'm working on right now...I can't say whether they're tears of happiness...or tears of non-happiness! I thought that I wanted Sven to love me, but now that he does…I just don't know what my feelings are feeling!"

"How 'bout if I cook you up a nice casserole?"

"Thanks, Lena, but I don't feel like burying my emotions under a big helping of your delicious casserole right now. I want to *feel* my emotions."

"But you're too darn skinny! You gotta put some meat on dem bones! Besides, the main way Swedish women express love is by cooking. So if anybody turns down my food, I don't feel like I'm being loved, ya?"

"Oh, so that's why most Swedish people are so big."

"Huh? No, it's everybody else dot is too small!"

"That's an interesting hypothesis," said Janet. "But now is the time for us to be discussing *my* screwed-up ideas of love. Maybe we can talk about *your* screwed-up ideas later."

"Ya shure," said Lena. "I mean, since you're the main character."

"Okay!" said Janet, tears welling up as she did a melodramatic arm-to-forehead-of-upturned-head-with-eyes-closed gesture. "Oh, why me? Why do I have to go fall in love with a weird Swedish boy who's out of touch with his emotions? He's totally the opposite of what I would have wanted! Why can't love be easy?"

"Janet," said Lena in a surrogate motherly way, "you don't have a choice about who you fall in love with. You only have a choice over how good you love."

"Wow, that's profound!" said Janet. "Do you mean I have a choice over the quality of my love? A choice of how pure or genuine it is? How unconditional? How free of contamination by my own personal issues and denial mechanisms? How accurately it reflects what the other person needs to fulfil their deep nature and grow as a person?"

"I don't know much 'bout dot," replied Lena. "I was talkin' about how good you be at makin' da whoopee."

Choosing to ignore that last comment, Janet went into an internal monologue.

What rotten timing, she thought to herself. *She finds a nice guy right on the verge of becoming a zombie. Could she tell him her secret? She had to! He deserved to hear the truth. On the other hand, he'd probably abandon her. And could she blame him? Actually, she could.*

On the other hand, what kind of future would they have together? A strapping young Swedish lad who uses language that sounds like it was from an old man, and an intellectual secular humanist teenage girl zombie! People would talk!

And they had such disparate interests, so little in common. He had such a wide variety of interests: fishing, talking about fishing, thinking about fishing, preparing gear for fishing, reading fishing magazines...the list went on and on.

On the other hand, her interests would soon coalesce into one interest: Brains!

On the other hand...wait, that's three hands. And she only had one! The other one was still being held by Hulda.

"Um, Hulda?" asked Janet politely, "Can you stick that back on? It could come in handy for playing Cat's Cradle."

"Ya shure," replied Hulda, "I chust sew it back on in a jiffy. Den you gotta git yerself some rest, ya? Then tomorrow—"

"Hey dere," said Ole, barging through the door. "What's goin' on?"

"Oh hello, Ole, "said Lena. "I'm just sewin' on Janet's arm."

"Okay, while you do that I'll have a heart-to-heart talk wit Janet."

"Hi temporary surrogate daddy," said Janet.

"I vant to tell you dot I don't trust this Sven character. He's not the sharpest tool in the shed."

"I don't care if his tools aren't sharp!" said Janet with a hint the defiant attitude she had used earlier in the story.

"Do you care that maybe he's a few bricks shy of a full load? That maybe he's playing solitaire without a full deck of cards?"

"Please, temporary surrogate daddy!" said Janet. "Let's talk openly and honestly without resorting to old-timey metaphors."

"Okay, dis is da ting," said Ole. "Dis kinda attraction is a first for you. In the coupla days I've known you, I've never seen you interested in a boy. And it ain't easy for me."

She hated the way he made his feelings for Sven make her feel like a slut. Actually, no—it was her *real* father that would have made her feel like a slut. Never mind.

"Janet, you're not just another hormone-driven melodramatic teenage girl."

"I'm not?"

"Of course not!" said Ole. "You're a *very special* hormone-driven melodramatic teenage girl. As your temporary surrogate father, I've been both anticipating and dreading this day for a coupla days. When I look at you, I still see the cute little ten-year-old girl that I never actually saw."

"I can send you a pic later," said Janet. "What's your email address?"

"It's ole.svenson@gmail.com. So to continue my speech, it's hard for me to accept that youse practically all grown up, nearly legal for havin' whoopee with. It's hard for me to accept you getting' involved with any man, even one who likes fishing."

"Oh, temporary surrogate daddy, I have questions that are too confusing for my young mind.

I need the wisdom of someone who has lived many years but is not yet dead."

"Well, I guess I am qualified for dot, ya?"

"Temporary surrogate daddy, I've been trying to figure out whether life makes any sense, or whether we're all floating around randomly in an uncaring universe. Why do people suffer even if they've done nothing to deserve it? How could a nice young teenager's life be destroyed for no good reason? Is life—and by extension, the universe—rational? Or is everything all topsy-turvy? Is life a cosmic joke? Or does it somehow make sense in some sort of cosmic 'big picture' that's beyond our ability to ever comprehend, hidden behind a veil that our human consciousness is unable to penetrate?"

"Um..." said a confused Ole. "I tink dose are questions for your surrogate mother. So as I was saying, I've been protecting you, keeping you safe, for the whole couple days of your life I've known you. And it's hard when it comes to da point where I can't protect you no more. It's like a father bird pushing the baby bird outta the nest and tells her, 'Fly, dammit! Fly or you'll hit da ground and da coyote will eat you.'"

"Oh, temporary surrogate daddy!"

"I just don't want you getting' eaten by no coyote. I vant to make sure dis Sven character ain't no coyote, ya?"

"Ya!" said Janet. "I mean, *yes!* Thanks, temporary surrogate daddy!"

"Okay Janet," said Lena, putting away her sewing kit. Da arm is all stuck back now. Youse can go now, but be careful for a coupla days, ya? No weightlifting or playin' roller derby for a while. Now skedaddle, and get some rest!"

"Thanks, surrogate mother!" said Janet, carefully making her way outside, slowly walking down the steps, until...

"Hi Janet!" said Aimee, running up to Janet with a bounce in her step and a smile on her lips and a sparkle in both of her eyes. "I have awesome news!"

"Tell me!"

"You were right about Nels. He *does* like me! He invited me to go on a canoe ride with him to the island in the middle of Lake Wichiganawaneehoohaw. It's called *Fornication Island.*"

"Really?" said Janet. "That's great! What do people do on *Fornication Island?*"

"You really are naïve, aren't you."

"Well, how would I know?" said Janet. "I've never been to Minnesota before."

"Have you ever been on a canoe ride, Janet?"

"No, I was raised in Southern Utah, remember? I've only seen photographs of canoe rides."

"Well, how about if you come along? You and Sven."

"Me and Sven?"

"Yes, it might be very 'romantic,' if you know what I mean," said Aimee, nudging Janet in the arm.

"Hey, easy on the arm! But as for the canoe ride, I think it sounds wonderful! I'll tell Sven all about it!"

CHAPTER 10

It had been sunny all morning, but suddenly the skies changed to overcast as clouds moved in from the North. If clouds could talk, they would have said, "Hey, we're clouds from the North, eh? It's aboot time we got here. Good day, eh?"

(They were Canadian clouds, get it?)

Janet was walking amidst the cabins, near the recreation center. Just *walking* this time, having abandoned previous attempts at such pretentious modes of locomotion as sauntering and meandering. As previously reported, she was a poor saunterer and an okay meanderer. She was, however, an excellent walkerer.

As for the clouds, they symbolized a dark turn in the story. They were... oh, what's the word? A portent? A foreshadowing?

Janet walked along, blissfully ignorant of whatever the right word is. But then she noticed something unusual was going on. She saw that Hulda, from the self-described cool and tough Njördsöň

Gang, was stapling something on every available surface: Cabin walls, trees, slow-moving guests. Then she noticed the other members of the gang doing the same thing, stapling something all over the place. It seemed to be posters of some kind. Groups of kids were reading the posters and laughing. All the Lake Wichiganawaneehoohaw Wayward Youth Recovery Camp subcultures were represented: the thugs, the drug burnouts, the former prostitutes and future prostitutes. The grungies were there. So were the punks, crunks, thunks, and the smiling young blonde girl wearing a unicorn rainbow t-shirt. Sadly, she was still a subculture with a population of only one. Poor little unicorn rainbow t-shirt girl.

Then an adorable little girl turned around and spotted Janet. She pointed at her and immediately began laughing an evil, sinister laugh. Or at least it seemed evil and sinister. Actually, it was a normal laugh. It just seemed evil and sinister coming from an adorable little girl.

Then other kids turned and pointed at her. And laughed.

They were laughing!

At!

Her!

Not laughing "with" her, since Janet was most definitely *not* laughing. She was wondering what in heck was on those posters. She was afraid to look. But she had to know!

She cautiously walked toward the nearest poster, which had been stapled to a woodpecker. And what she saw was...*OH NO!* It was worse than she could have possibly imagined! She was horrified! Someone had Photoshopped an image of her face onto the body of a supermodel on a Hawaiian beach, wearing only a pair of Victoria's Secret bikini-thong panties and a carefully positioned flower lei.

She was surrounded by kids who were laughing uncontrollably. They were pointing at Janet and saying things like, "You look purdy good underneath dose clothes!" and "I didn't know a secular humanist could be so hot!" and a solemn, whispered "Can we go on a date?" from the unicorn rainbow t-shirt girl. Who would have thought!

But Janet didn't have time for thinking; she was too busy being horrified. Because as she looked at a few more posters, she saw that they each had text under the photo.

JANET WILL SPIN YOUR PICKLE ANY TIME

JANET NEVER SAYS NO TO A KOSHER DILL

IF YOU NEED A PLACE TO HIDE YOUR PICKLE, CALL JANET

And it went on like this, a series of really stupid pickle/penis double-entendres—composed by kids who surely didn't even understand what the word *double-entendre* means.

But once again, Janet was too busy to consider how such a thing is even possible, since she was too busy FREAKING OUT. Surrounded by gangs of kids pointing their cruel little fingers at her and laughing their stupid little heads off. Or perhaps their fingers were stupid and their heads were cruel?

If this was a movie, Janet's emotional state would be suggested by adding echo effects to the laughter, and by the visual special effect of having multiple, overlapping close-ups of the laughing faces of the cruel children. This isn't an effect you see too much nowadays, but was very popular in the 1950s and earlier. An excellent example of this effect can be seen in the 1927 silent film classic *Metropolis*, an expressionist dystopian sci-fi directed by Fritz Lang.

The film stands up remarkably well to modern audiences—even the special effects which were decades ahead of their time. The film was basically the first appearance of the archetypal "mad scientist" that was to become a mainstay of movies up to this day. The original *Frankenstein* (1931, directed by James Whale) basically ripped-off the entire laboratory scene. The only aspect of the film that doesn't translate well to modern audiences is the expressionistic acting style, which seems to us—who are accustomed to a more "naturalistic" style—stilted and exaggerated.

Okay... back to our story, and to our protagonist Janet who most assuredly is not "acting" here. Her confusion and anguish and terror are not exaggerated. She is truly having a bad hair day.

"LEAVE ME ALONE!" she shrieked. "WHY ARE YOU BEING SO MEAN TO ME? WHY?"

"BECAUSE," shouted an angry male Swedish voice, "DEY IS NOT VERY NICE, YA?"

It was Sven!

The second he appeared the kids stopped laughing, especially the members of The Njördsön Gang who stopped laughing the most.

"Uf da!" said Hjalmar, starting to slink away, "I tink I gots to be somewhere right 'bout now."

"HOLD IT RIGHT THERE YOU HOOLIGAN!" thundered Sven, who would have shot a bolt of lightning if he know how.

Hjalmar stopped in his tracks, as did the other members of The Njördsön Gang. The other kids cleared out of the way as Sven slowly walked toward the gang, like a scene out of *High Noon* or some other Western movie with a big shootout scene on the main street. But this was Minnesota, not Wyoming or Colorado, and although there have been many movie *Westerns* there has never been a movie called a *Northern*.

The members of The Njördsön Gang were suddenly thinking how they'd rather be drinking hot cocoa and hugging their blankies as their mommies tucked them into bed. They began shaking in fear as the fearsome Sven slowly bore down on them. The gang members were of one mind in their desire to scapegoat each other in their desire to escape *The Wrath of Sven* (doesn't that sound like the title of a movie?).

"Who made dese tings?" asked Sven menacingly, indicating the naughty posters with a wide sweep of his Swedish arms.

"I did the Photoshop work," volunteered Hulda, seeing her opportunity to escape. "But Lars did the art direction."

"Did not!" protested Lars.

"Okey-dokey Hulda," said Sven. "Youse is declared innocent."

"Awesome, Sven!" said Hulda, "Tanks a lot!"

Then Sven's iron gaze focused on Lars, who began shaking uncontrollably.

"So," said Sven. "Youse did the art direction, ya?"

"Um..." quivered Lars, searching amidst his panicked mind for a scapegoat, which really shouldn't have been too hard since the only one left to blame was...

"Hjalmar made me do it!" said Lars.

"Did not!" yelled Hjalmar.

"I warned him," said Lars. "I tried to tell him, 'Hjalmar I don't tink I'm good at da art directing ting, ya?"

"Okey-dokey Lars," said Sven. "Youse is declared innocent."

"Tanks, Sven!" said Lars, then to himself said, "Uf-da, dot was a close vun!"

Hjalmar's mind raced in circles for a scapegoat he could blame to secure his freedom. Unfortunately for him, he was running out of scapegoats. He had only one option.

"Hjalmar made me do it," said Hjalmar.

Sven's mind paused for only the tiniest fraction of a second, then plowed ahead.

"Oh yeah?" said Sven. "Dis Hjalmar sounds like a real *bad apple*. He probably needs to be *peeled and cored*, ya?"

"Oh ya!" agreed a suddenly very relieved Hjalmar. "If I ever get my hands on dis Hjalmer character... Uf-da! He's gonna be sorry, ya?"

"Well," pondered Sven, "it's a good ting The Njördsöň Gang ain't responsible for dese bad posters, ya?"

"Oh ya!" said The Njördsöň Gang in three-part harmony.

"So I betcha The Njördsöň Gang will take down dese bad posters and burn 'em up in da fire pit, ya?"

"You betcha!" said The Njördsöň Gang.

As they meekly removed the posters, the crowd dispersed to the fire pit. Soon, the big gang of kids were enjoying themselves as they watched the members of The Njördsöň Gang take turns setting the new kids on fire.

Janet and Sven were left alone to make google-eyes at each other.

"Oh Sven," swooned Janet. "My hero!"

"It vas about time somebody taught dot gang a ting or two!"

"Oh Sven, I think it's time for us to reveal our true feelings toward each other."

"Well, dot's okay. As long as we don't hafta talk about emotions, ya?"

"Oh Sven, I know that, as a Swede, emotions are hard for you. But I need to tell you what my emotions are feeling right now. It's hard to put into words. It's kind of like the wind. I can't see it, but I can feel it."

"Huh?"

"Sven, I'm talking about the word *love*."

"I tot you said it was hard to put into words?"

"Sven... I love you, Sven. How do you feel about me?"

"Oh Janet, I... lo...lu..."

"C'mon, Sven! I know you can do it!"

"I lou...lar..."

"Keep trying, Sven!"

Then Sven cried out in anguish and collapsed, grasping his head with his strong Swedish hands.

"That's okay, Sven. Thanks for trying! I know what you mean, even if the word gets stuck in your brain."

"Tanks!" said an exhausted Sven. "Dot wore me out."

"Wait..." said Janet. "I told you something long ago, when we first met last Tuesday. I told you not to fall in love with me."

"Huh? I tot you wanted me to fall in... lo... lar..."

"Sven! There's something I need to tell you...but I can't! Not yet! I don't want to destroy this beautiful and precious moment, this special feeling."

"Maybe you can tell me tomorrow, ya?"

"What's tomorrow?"

"Don't cha remember? Tomorrow's da big canoe trip with Aimee and Nels. Maybe you can tell me then, ya?"

"Maybe Sven," said Janet, glancing into the darkening sky as sparks from a burning kid floated towards the heavens, "maybe."

CHAPTER 11

It was a perfect summer day on the shore of Lake Wichiganawaneehoohaw. It was such a perfect and beautiful day that the mosquitos decided to take a day off. This gave wholesome teens the opportunity to pursue good clean summer fun without constantly swatting their arms or being smothered in DEET. Yes, wholesome teens had the opportunity to pursue good clean summer fun such as a canoe ride to Fornication Island.

As Sven and Nels were loading blankets and coolers into the canoe, Janet and Aimee had a brief giggly conversation.

"Janet!" asked Aimee excitedly. "How's it going with you and Sven?"

"Oh, Aimee! It's going wonderfully. He told me he don't mind me hangin' around!"

"What's it like being in love?"

"Oh, how can I possibly describe it?" said Janet, pausing to gaze into the bright blue sky while searching for just the right words. What was she thinking, that words float around in the sky for you to pick and choose?

"It's like cute puppies," she continued, "with waggy little tails and strawberry ice cream with a cherry on top!"

"Janet?" said Aimee, who was also having trouble finding the right words. "I know you're from Southern Utah, but are you freaking kidding me?"

"Aimee, watch your language!" scolded Janet. "We're supposed to be wholesome teens having good clean summer fun!"

"Hey you two," shouted Nels, "the canoe is ready for us wholesome teens to head out for some good clean summer fun."

Janet boarded the canoe, followed by Aimee and Nels. Standing on the dock was Sven, steadying the canoe with his strong Swedish hands which were firmly attached to his strong Swedish torso by his strong Swedish arms. Sven yelled "All aboard, ya?" which made everybody laugh, signifying that they were having fun (of the good clean summer variety, of course).

Off they went across the sun-dappled waters of Lake Wichiganawaneehoohaw—Janet and Sven cozy in the front, Aimee and Nels even more cozy in the back. In order to avoid sexist stereotypes, Sven and Nels relaxed while the girls did all the paddling.

Wait a minute...is that "avoiding sexist stereotypes"? Or is it "making women do all the work"?

Nels was looking cuter than ever. His luscious brown hair was tousled by the breeze and wavering across his sensuous forehead, gently tickling the welts from yesterday's mosquito bites before the filthy little bloodsuckers took the day off. He couldn't take his gorgeous green eyes off Aimee's smiling face, mainly because his view was blocked from Aimee's butt.

"Hey Aimee," said Nels, playing at being an innocent teen having good clean fun, but not succeeding too well, "did you bring any *protection?*"

"Yes!" said Aimee. "Can't you see that I'm wearing a life jacket?"

They all laughed, signifying...well, you get the idea by now.

As Janet and Sven rejoiced in the warm glow of the sun, Aimee and Nels rejoiced in the warm glow of flowing hormones. Aimee was unable to resist Nels' sensuous forehead, and soon her hands were caressing his mosquito welts.

"Hey Sven," said Aimee. "Could you take over paddling for me? My hands are currently occupied with another project."

"Ya, no problem," said Sven.

"And in a related request," said Nels, "could you and Janet remain looking forward and not turn around? By the way, this request has nothing to do with the chance that you might accidentally see some partial wholesome teen nudity back here."

"And possibly," added Aimee, "some softcore wholesome teen foreplay."

"No problem!" replied Janet. "This will give me and Sven a chance to do more bonding."

In the back of the canoe, things were getting...oh, let's say they were getting very *wholesome*.

Janet turned to Sven and asked, "Sven, do you ever get tired of fishing? I mean, it looks so easy for you. Like it's not a challenge for you anymore. And as we all know, a life without challenge is an empty life devoid of meaning."

"Well, dot's why I do more than just catchin' fish."

"Oh Sven, that's great. I didn't realize you had interests outside of fishing. Do you paint? Perhaps you write? Maybe not poetry, but perhaps very masculine Hemmingway-esque tales of the rugged Northern life. Perhaps you play a musical instrument? What else do you do besides catching fish?"

"I wrestle 'em."

"Huh? Fish wrestling? People actually wrestle fish?"

"Aren't you going to ask me if I'm afraid of getting hurt?"

"Actually," said Janet, "that wasn't what I was going to—"

"It yust goes wit da sport, ya? If youse wrestle da fish you might get stuck with the spines. Or bit by the sharp teeth. Or slimed with fish slime."

"Yuck!"

"You can watch some fish wrestlin' real soon. Dere's a fish wrestlin' contest comin' up here at camp. It's the big highlight at the end of *Lutefisk Days*. Dot's the big end-of-summer party."

"*Lutefisk?*" asked Janet. "What's that?"

"Lutefisk is a traditional Swedish meal. It's made of fish soaked in lye for two days, then wrapped in cheesecloth and boiled."

"That sounds...um..." said Janet, searching for a way to sound diplomatic. "That sounds *interesting*."

"It's delicious!" said Sven. "You'll love it. It tastes like warm fish-flavored Jell-O."

"Oh!" said a fast-thinking Janet. "I'm allergic to that. My doctor said that if I eat even one bite of anything that tastes like warm fish-flavored Jell-O, I'll break out in chives."

"Don't you mean *hives?*"

"No, chives," replied Janet, who refused to admit that she made an incorrect word choice. "Little green onions that can be used in salads."

The canoe reached the shoreline of Fornication Island, its bow sliding gently into the sand in the shallow waters of the beach. Sven leapt from the canoe, not tipping it over at all, and kept it steady with his strong Swedish hands. Janet happily jumped off the canoe, landing in a few inches of cool water that felt so good on her naked 17-year-old toes. She felt the unfamiliar sensation of being...what's the word? She felt *sexy!* And just a little bit *naughty.* Here she was, on a wilderness island. With a boy. And her toes were naked!

She turned to help Aimee and Nels out of the canoe, and they... Where did they go? Oh—there they are, running hand-in-hand to the other side of the island on a trail through a grove of tall woody things.

"Hey Sven?" asked Janet. "What do you suppose they're going to do on the other side of Fornication Island?"

"Um..." said Sven, knowing full well what two hormonal teenagers were going to do on the other side of Fornication Island. But wanting to preserve Janet's youthful naïveté, he said, "I tink dey are gonna do some arm wrestling."

"How about us, Sven? What we are we going to do here, all alone, on the shore of Fornication Island, all alone, with nobody watching us? I feel like doing something a little bit crazy. I feel like getting wild, doing something I've never done before. What should we do?"

"I know," said Sven, knowing that this scene had to stay G-rated, "let's do a movie montage!"

"Really? Oh, that would make me so happy! I've never done a movie montage! It's a little scary, but I think I'm ready. But Sven, I have one request."

"Sure."

"Be gentle. It's my first montage."

"Ya shure!" said Sven. "The movie montage is always G-rated."

Cue the soundtrack, which is a bouncy pop song by an up-and-coming indie rock band. No need to specify the band or the name of the song, because it's the same generic movie montage song you've heard a million times before.

MONTAGE SCENE ONE

Janet and Sven running along the beach, hand-in-hand, laughing joyfully, loving this moment, loving each other's company, not a care in the world. But the beach is only 30 feet long so they have to turn around and come back the other way. Cut scene before they get winded and Sven has to run into the woods to pee.

FADE TO MONTAGE SCENE TWO

Janet is lying on her back on the beach, and Sven is outlining her with seashells. Yes, there are no seashells in Northern Minnesota, but what are you going to do? Have Sven outline her with rocks?

FADE TO MONTAGE SCENE THREE

Suddenly Janet is wearing her blue Reeboks for this very emotionally endearing scene. Sven is suddenly holding a Sharpie pen, and is writing on one of her Reeboks the words "I don't mind you hangin' around." On the other Reebok he attempts to draw a heart, but it comes out looking like a fish. They laugh and laugh and laugh.

"Wow!" said Janet. "What a great movie montage! So much better than real life!"

"Ya! Because dey edit out all the boring stuff, like when I had to go to the woods to pee, and when we had to go back to camp to get your Reeboks and a Sharpie pen. Dey only keep in the most fun little parts, but in real life you gotta do all da udder stuff, too."

"Oh Sven, this day has been so wonderful! I wish that..."

Janet's words trailed off as she heard some unusual sounds coming from the other side of Fornication Island. Strange sounds. Primal sounds. Moans and groans. Like something was in pain.

"Sven!" said a worried Janet. "Do you hear that? What is it? I'm scared! It sounds like wild animals!"

"Um..." said Sven, knowing full well once again what was happening on the other side of Fornication Island. But wanting once again to preserve Janet's youthful naïveté, he said, "It's just a coupla *bears*."

"But Aimee and Nels are over there arm wrestling! We need to save them."

"Oh, it's no problem," said Sven, wanting once again to etc. etc., "Bears get excited watching people arm wrestle. When da wrestlin' is over, da bears will go back to eating berries."

Then from the other side of the island came the voice of Aimee shouting, "YES! YES!"

"Sounds like Aimee won," said Janet.

"Ya, I guess you could put it like dot."

"Oh Sven," said Janet. "I think Aimee and Nels have fallen in love!" And we are having so much fun together."

"Ya, tings is looking not too bad."

"Oh Sven, you're happy too!" said Janet, giving Sven a big hug. Then she realized she wanted to give him something else. No, not that! If that's what you thought, then you have a dirty mind. What she really wanted to give him was...

"A present!" she announced, handing Sven a big box covered in wrapping paper with images of all Minnesota game fish.

"Oh, dot's great!" said a smiling Sven. "Yoost vat I always vanted, a box with pictures of fish."

"Um, Sven? The present is on the *inside* of the box."

"Oh, d'ya mean dere's *more?*"

"Ya!" said Janet. "I mean, *yes.* Open the box!"

Sven obliged. Because why wouldn't he? He smiled as he slowly removed the paper, careful not to tear any of the fish pictures. It would be bad fishing luck, he reasoned. But he came close to tearing the head off the Walleye. Close call! He was very careful when he encountered the Muskie, the most ferocious game fish in Minnesota, because he didn't want to risk losing a finger. Does that sound superstitious? Consider that muskies have been known to attack and kill ducks that were swimming peacefully along the surface of lakes and, in one famous incident, leapt out of the water and took down a low-flying airplane.

"Hey Sven," said Janet with a playful twinkle in her eyes, "wake me up when you get finished okay?"

"Uf-da! Am I dot slow?"

Half an hour later, he woke up Janet.

"Okay now," he said, "I'm about to open da box."

"Is it still today?" asked Janet, without a playful twinkle in her eye.

"Let's see what's inside!" said Sven, opening the box to reveal...

"A fishing reel!"

"Yes!" said Janet, who was positively glowing at this point. "It's a Shimano® Symetre Spinning Reel, which is supposed to be the best reel on the market. Long a favorite with spinning-reel anglers, the Symetre now has even more to like with improvements that include Shimano's M compact body design for weight reduction, Propulsion® Line Management System that delivers trouble-free, tangle-free casting, and Varispeed 11 oscillation for even line lay and long casts."

"Oh, tank you Janet!"

"Should I also tell you about the Propulsion spool lip that provides longer casting distances while preventing backlashes, and the S-Rotor that ensures a comfortable retrieve?"

"Dot's fine, you can stop now."

"Oh, and maybe there's more in the box?" said Janet playfully. "I think maybe I see something else down there."

"Oh really?" said Sven. He dug around underneath some crumpled newspaper and found...what was this thing? It had a cover. And inside the cover were sheets of paper. And on the sheets of paper were markings of some kind. In other words, it was...

"A book!" shouted Sven, suddenly not happy. He looked at the markings on the cover. The title was, *The Ontology of Ideas Implicit within Critiques of Postmodern Social Theory.*

"It's my favorite book!" said Janet, still glowing so positively that she didn't notice Sven's smile had faded into a grumpy frown. "It will expand your mind! I can't wait for you to read it! Then we can have intellectual conversations about whether deconstructionism has gone too far in its rejection of all philosophical frameworks rather than merely inspiring careful examination of the assumptions within those frameworks."

"Janet?" asked a decidedly unsmiling Sven. "Are you saying dot I am not smart? Dot I need to be edumecated?"

"Oh no, Sven!" said Janet, starting to panic. "You just haven't been exposed to someone who is willing to expand your knowledge beyond fishing."

"All my life, people been callin' me stupid. They talk behind my back. Or sometimes in front of my back."

"Oh Sven, I didn't mean to imply that—"

"But when dey talk in front of my back, dey don't realize I can see 'em, ya? Dot's because dey tink Sven's stupid. Dey tink Sven's not the sharpest tool in the shed. Dey tink he's a few bricks shy of a full load. Dey tink he's playin' solitaire without a full deck of cards."

"Please, Sven! I didn't realize—"

"I tot you liked me just for being me," said Sven, staring straight into Janet's eyes, his piercing blue eyes as cold as two cans of PBR fresh out of the refrigerator.

"I'm not going to attempt to reply," said Janet, "because you're probably going to cut me off just like–"

"But I guess you only like me if I'm somebody else."

"Are you done yet? Because—"

"You intellectual city-slicker girls are all alike! You tink you can buy my brains with money and stuff it full of smarts."

"Sven! That's not true! Also, that's probably the weirdest sentence I've ever heard."

"You said that you...you know—the 'L' word—about me. But if you don't L-word me as I am, den I don't tink you can L-word me at all. Goodbye, Janet. It hos been some fun, but it's all over for us."

An awkward silence fell between them. A tiny cloud suddenly appeared and cast a shadow on exactly the spot they were standing on.

"Okay," he added. "You can say a speech now."

But Janet was not capable of speech. She wasn't capable of thinking. She could barely even breathe. Fortunately, her brain stem continued her lung function, as well as her other metabolic activities. Including her tear ducts, which were working *very* well. Also her legs, which she used to run back to the lodge.

Generally speaking, it was not an unusual scene: Jilted girlfriend is upset and runs back to a safe sanctuary. Of course, what made it unusual is that they were on an island and the "safe sanctuary" was back on shore. Good thing Janet is a very fast runner.

CHAPTER 12

The next day dragged for Janet. Then six more days dragged, making it a very draggy week. She felt listless and weak and unwell. Her nose ran and her feet smelled. Was she turning upside down?

To symbolize her inner emotional state, the weather for Northern Minnesota was cold and rainy, with the cold symbolizing her feelings and the rain symbolizing her tears. Have you noticed how the weather always seem to symbolize the emotional state of the main character? So for now the forecast was cold and rainy, but a warm front from the South was expected to bring sunny skies as soon as Janet cheered up.

But that did not seem to happening anytime soon. This pissed off the people organizing the upcoming Lutefisk Days, because they were counting on decent weather.

Janet spent days moping in her cabin. Then she got sick of moping in her cabin and decided that moping in the main lodge would be a delightful change of scene. Also, people could see that she was in a mopey mood, whereas when she was in her cabin they just thought *Where's Janet?*

She proved to be an excellent moper. Lost in her own mopiness, she totally ignored the kids gathered around the television watching cartoon animals blow each other up and push each other into vats of acid.

If only she could forget Sven. But it was hard...so very hard. Reminders of him were everywhere. On the coat rack was a kid that Sven hung there last week by his collar, still squirming helplessly in hopes that someone will let him down. She gazed upon her blue Reeboks, where Sven wrote the words "I don't mind you hangin' around"—but the writing had faded... just like their love had faded. Janet cried as she remembered the first time Sven tried to say the words "I love you" and nearly had a brain hemorrhage.

There was an image of Sven that kept coming to her, kept sneaking into her consciousness, kept galloping across the canvas of her memory. It was an image from the first time she realized Sven was okey-dokey. It was the image of Sven standing beside the lake with his big ten-inch trout.

The image made her cry, because it reminded her of something that once felt so good, but she could never have again. She would never have Sven. Or his trout.

Where was he, anyway? Probably off flirting with the dumbest girl he could find. It made Janet want to cry. But she realized that moping and crying don't really go together. A person that's moping doesn't care enough to cry. She decided to stick with the long-term rewards of moping, and not give in to the short-term satisfaction of crying.

Suddenly, Janet felt a warm happy hand holding her cold mopey hand. She looked up to see the smiling face of Aimee.

"Janet," she said, "as your best friend forever, I can't bear to see you moping around like this."

"Really?"

"Yes. Also, you need to cheer up enough to bring good weather for Lutefisk Days tomorrow."

"I only wish I could," said Janet in the most mopey way possible. "But I don't love myself enough to cheer up."

"Well," said Aimee. "Then do it for me. Remember when you told me about your philosophy of life?"

"You mean, *the only way to fulfil myself is by fulfilling others?*"

"Yes, and I thought you were talking about sexual fulfillment. Which is true, by the way. I mean, as long as the other person follows through and fulfills you back. But in your case, we're talking about something deeper and more meaningful than sex."

"We are?"

"Yes! So as your best friend forever, you *must* accompany me to Lutefisk Days tomorrow. And I order you to quit moping immediately. The field needs to dry out overnight for all the games we want to play."

"Well, okay," said Janet, the faintest hint of a smile coming to her face. "I'll do it for you, my best friend forever!"

The next day Janet was feeling cool and overcast, with only a ten-percent chance of light crying. Lutefisk Days was on! The field was full of kids playing tug-of-war, kids having sack races, and kids avoiding the table where Lena was trying to serve plates of warm lutefisk. The air was alive with the laughter of children and the buzzing of mosquitos, reinvigorated by the rainy weather and out for blood. The mosquitos, I mean—not the children.

It was a perfect day for fish wrestling. Or at least as perfect for fish wrestling as any day could be. Janet was sitting on the bleachers next to Aimee, lost in her own sadness. A tear started forming in Janet's left eye. Not wanting to be left out, her right eye also formed a tear.

Janet was jolted out of her thoughts by Aimee. "Hey Janet, is something the matter?"

"Oh, nothing," lied Janet, "just something in my eyes...something that's salty but isn't tears."

"Oh, it must be salted peanuts," said Aimee. "Hey, isn't this fish wrestling contest exciting?"

"Oh yes!" said Janet, telling the truth for a change, "I never suspected those underwater puppies would put up such a fight!"

"Oh Janet!" laughed Aimee. "You are so funny!"

"Aimee, I was just wondering about something. I was thinking about all that 'living in the moment' stuff you were talking about. It made a lot of sense to me, but then I started thinking that maybe it's good to live for the future, too."

"Um..." said Aimee, nervously, "you're not questioning my underlying belief system, are you?"

"For example," continued Janet, "when I go grocery shopping I like to buy for a week at a time. Otherwise, if I lived for the moment it would be like, 'Oh, I'm hungry again. Better run down to the store for an apple.'"

"Rather than questioning my basic existential outlook that provides metaphysical meaning, let's watch fish wrestling!"

"Okay! Boy, the Svens haven't been doing well, have they."

"It looks like all the Svens have lost to the Northern Pikes. Not only did they lose the wrestling matches, but each Sven also lost at least one finger."

"Hey, why do only *boys* get to wrestle fishes? Why not the girls? Is Camp Wichiganawaneehoohaw *sexist?*"

"No, it's not that. It's because girls are smart."

The fish wrestling contest was nearly over, only one more contestant. And of course, it was...

"Sven!" cried Janet. "I can't believe it!"

"Janet," teased Aimee, "you're not still *emotionally involved*, are you?"

Before Janet could reply in some bitchy smart-ass way, a bell sounded and all eyes turned to the water. Sven stood boldly in one corner, even though lakes don't have corners. In the other non-existent corner, the water bubbled menacingly. Sven pounded his chest and shouted, "I tink tonight fer supper I'll have me some *Nordern Pike!*"

He tore off his shirt, revealing a muscular torso and sculpted abs. A thin sheen of sweat glistened in the overcast, highlighting his firm six-pack abs. Actually, it looked like an eight-pack. No wait...was it a twelve-pack? Is that possible? How many ribs is a person supposed to have?

His hair suddenly became ruffled in a very "bedroom-friendly" sexy hairstyle, suggesting Johnny Depp in the movie *Cry-Baby*.

"Sigh..." Janet sighed. "Such a good looking guy. Too bad nothing could possibly happen to ever get us together again."

From the menacing bubbles leapt a monster fish—a Northern Pike over three feet long, with teeth like white daggers and a bad attitude.

"Gasp!" the crowd gasped.

"Oh no!" Janet oh-no'd.

The monster pike splashed back into the water, and only a massive fin protruded above the surface, making a rapid course straight for Sven. The crowd was too busy gasping for anyone to make the ominous "da dum...da dum" music from the movie *Jaws*.

As Sven considered whether this whole fish wrestling thing was a good idea, the monster fish leapt from the water right toward his face, trying to decide which of his piercing blue eyes to aim for.

"Not my piercing blue eyes!" shouted Sven, with a sudden rise of anger and testosterone. "Hey, I tink you go really gud wit *hash brown potatoes!*"

Just as the monster pike was about to munch on Sven's left eye, since it had decided that the right eye didn't look as tasty, Sven turned his head to the side like in a Bruce Lee movie where Bruce Lee turns his head to barely avoid one of those thrown pointed-star things.

With lightning reflexes and thunderous nerves, Sven reached out and snatched the monster pike by the gills. The pike's momentum brought them both crashing into the water, into a broiling blood-filled cauldron of foam and splashing sounds. The crowd had grown too stunned to gasp, and were quietly discussing whether it would be more appropriate to be petrified in silence or to shriek in terror.

After a long minute which seemed even more longer, Sven burst from the foaming water holding the thrashing pike tightly around its neck, and stumbled toward the beach. The crowd decided that at this time it would be appropriate to cheer.

"Go Sven! Show that pike who's boss!"

"Teach that fish a lesson!"

One of the Svens shouted, "Could you reach inside its mouth and see if my finger is still there?"

Motivated by the crowd's cheers, Sven had the pike pinned to the sandy beach. It thrashed with its spiny tail and sliced into Sven's arms, causing red streaks of blood just like with Bruce Lee in the movie *Enter the Dragon*.

Just as Sven was about to deliver the fatal squeeze that would strangle the monster pike and put an end to its reign of fishy terror, the pike began singing: *I'm on the top of the world / looking down on creation.*

Sven gasped in surprise. The crowd gasped in surprise. The Northern Pike had been through all this, so it did not gasp in surprise.

Suddenly the pike was addressing Sven in a man's voice: "Janet, I arrived in Duluth this morning and I'm on my way there. I'll be at the camp in a couple of hours."

Sven turned and shouted to Janet, "Hey Janet, it's for you!"

The confusion caused Sven to loosen his grip on the monster pike, and the enraged fish took advantage of the moment to summon all its strength in a final lunge toward Sven's forehead, sinking a circle of sharp dagger-like teeth deeply into his flesh, through his skull, and into his brain.

"Ouch," said Sven.

Seizing the opportunity, the monster pike wriggled through the sand into the water, then stood upright on its tail fin and turned to address the crowd. Except that fish can't talk, even though the pike was understandably confused at this point. Unable to do anything, the slightly disappointed pike shrugged and wriggled back into the water and swam off.

"Sven!" shouted Janet, running to the beach. "Are you all right?"

"No problem," said Sven, "Just a flesh wound. Also, bones and brain, eh?"

Then his piercing blue eyes rolled upward toward his piercing red forehead wounds, and he collapsed unconscious.

CHAPTER 13

The next day, in a very touching and emotional scene, Janet appeared in Sven's cabin. Sven was reclining in bed, with fresh bandages on his many wounds.

"Oh, Sven!" she said in a very touching and emotional way, "Thank goodness you're all right!"

"Oh ya!" said Sven, proudly, "I really showed dot fish a ting or two, ya?"

"Well, not to get too technical about it," she said, "but the fish won."

"Ya, but I came in second place!"

Rather than point out that, in a contest between two opponents, second place is last place, Janet decided to change the subject.

"Sven, why are you so out-of-touch with your feelings? I mean, besides being Swedish."

"Vell, I had to shut down to protect myself."

"Oh, this is good. I just love this melodramatic stuff!" said Janet with glee.

"Hey, stop being so gleeful, ya? This ain't easy for me."

"Sorry!"

"Okay den. I had to shut down because last time I had a feeling it hurt me in my emotions. Something horrible happened to my mom. It was... a *zombie!*"

"A zombie? What happened?"

"Oh Janet, don't make me feel dose feelings again!"

"Was she eaten by a zombie?"

"No, she died from food poisoning when a zombie served her undercooked pork."

"Oh Sven!" she said, while little red hearts danced over her head. "That touching and heartfelt confession makes me feel closer to you."

"It made me feel less Swedish."

"Oh, just look at you!" she said brightly, brushing aside her sensible brown hair, "Without your clothes, you're naked!"

"Uf-da, you are shure enough right about dot!" he offered, "But I don't understand why to fix my head Hulda had to take off my pants."

"Oh, you know doctors," said Janet, "they really need to do a full examination in order to arrive at an accurate prognosis. The human body is an interconnected system of *parts*."

And with the mention of *parts* (italicized) she found herself getting warm for some reason.

"I suppose," offered Sven, "dot I should be puttin' on some pants, ya?"

"Why, y-yes," stammered Janet, "I mean...I s-suppose you're getting chilled."

"Actually," said Sven, "I tink it's getting' kinda *warm* in here...now dot *you're* here."

Sven struggled to put on his pants, groaning with effort. Janet had never heard groaning before, and it was exciting her for some reason. Janet had grown up in St. George, and had only seen photographs of groaning.

"Uf-da!" he said, frustrated, "My poor ol' body is too stiff from wrestlin' dot fish. I can't even put on my own pants."

"Let me help you," said Janet, whose body temperature had risen five degrees and whose sensible brown hair was suddenly much less sensible. She grasped his Levi™ blue jeans, whose rough surface contrasted with the smooth white skin of Sven's legs. She noticed they were hairy—his legs, not the blue jeans. She slipped the jeans over his strong Swedish feet...with such manly well-developed toes. There were no annoying corns or blisters. The nails were neatly trimmed, which made her heart begin to beat faster.

She slowly slid the blue jeans up his lower legs, then over the kneecaps, then up his muscular thighs. She tried hard to avert her eyes from what came next, although her peripheral vision sensed that it was large. Her heart started beating louder and louder, and she thought surely he would be able to hear it. But she thought that would be ridiculous.

"Nice strong heartbeat!" said Sven.

Janet grew lightheaded and was afraid she was going to pass out. "I think I should go back to my cabin to sort out my recycling," she was barely able to say.

He suddenly got serious, and looked into her eyes with those piercing blue eyes of his. "Or you could fergit all about da recycling" he murmured, "und see if yur pants kin come off, too."

"Huh?" replied a naïve and innocent Janet, who—as has been made very clear by now—had never lived outside of St. George.

"You know," hinted Sven, "conjugal relations, the horizontal dance, the beast with two backs."

"What?" said Janet, whose once-charming naïveté was wearing thin.

"Making whoopee!" cried Sven.

"Oh, you mean *sex!*" said Janet. Then she went off into an internal monologue.

Making whoopee, thought Janet. *On one hand, No of course not! On the other hand, Sure why not? On the other hand...wait, she was out of hands again.*

Also, she was running out of time. If she didn't seize this opportunity, she may never have another. She longed to experience what it would be like to lower herself down onto him, her hands grasping his manly Swedish torso as she enveloped his large Swedish member with her special place. It would be kinda cool to experience the sensation of being filled with a large Swedish member, at least once.

But what if during the delicate act of love she turned into a zombie? He would be defenseless against the fatal bite that would turn him into a fellow member of the living dead. And what if she ate his brains?

Is there such a thing as 'safe sex' for zombies? Maybe she could wear a hockey face mask? Would Sven be into that? Maybe it would be a turn-on? Even then, it would be risky. Even if it was only one chance in a million, that would be too much to risk. But what if it was only one chance in a billion? Hmm...

But no. She did not have a good enough knowledge of statistical analysis to deduce the risk within an acceptable degree of certainty.

She knew her answer, and with that knowledge she began to cry. She cried only one tear, but it was a way big tear.

"No thanks!" she told Sven.

"Huh?" replied Sven, "Are you still here? Sorry, I guess I dozed off."

"But because of our deep and genuine love for each other, I feel that you deserve to know why. Thus, you will be the first person to whom I reveal my deep, dark secret. Pretty cool, huh?"

"What's your name again?"

"Sven...I'm turning into a zombie."

"Really? Well ain't dot sometin!"

Janet stared silently as Sven continued smiling his goofy smile. There was the sound of crickets in the distance.

"Um...Sven? I realize you're not in touch with your emotional core, but shouldn't you be...um...*shocked* or something?"

"Wait until you hear *my* deep, dark secret. I'm 178 years old."

"What?" said a stunned Janet. The sound of distant crickets returned.

After an appropriate amount of shocked silence, she said, "Is that possible?"

After pondering for a few moments, she added, "Actually, that would explain why you talk like an old man. It would also explain why you didn't get my references to 80s music."

"I love da music from the 80s!"

"But you didn't get my references to *Duran Duran!*"

"Who?"

"That's just what I mean!"

"Janet, I like da music from the *1880s!* You know, ragtime. Scott Joplin."

"Who?"

"Dey sure don't make music like that no more. I don't like any music after 1920. It all went downhill from dere. Dot crazy *jazz* music wrecked everyting."

"But if you're 178 years old, why do you look so young?"

"Oh, dots because I discovered da Fountain of Youth!"

"The Fountain of Youth? It really exists? Wow! There are many legends, of course, about the existence of a body of water that restores the youth of anyone who drinks of it or bathes in its waters. Tales of such a fountain have been recounted in myths and stories for thousands of years, from the writings of Herodotus in the 5th century BC, up through the indigenous people of the Caribbean during the Age of Exploration. The legend of The Fountain of Youth gained worldwide fame as a result of the Spanish explorer Juan Ponce de León, first Governor of Puerto Rico. He was searching for the Fountain of Youth when he travelled to what is now Florida in 1513."

"But he didn't find it."

"How do you know that, Sven? Did you read the Wikipedia entry?"

"Huh? No, I know he didn't find it because I know where it really is."

"Tell me, Sven!"

"It's just north of here. It's called Leech Lake."

"Ewww!" said a grimacing Janet. "Gross! How can you bathe in a lake full of leeches?"

"No, dot's just da name," said Sven. "The ting of it is, dere's no leeches in it at all. That name is just to scare off city slickers, ya?"

"Oh, I get it! Sven, that was a brilliant idea!"

"It wasn't my idea. It was the idea of da two women I found dere."

"Two women? Sven, it makes me jealous to hear you mention *women*. That implies *other women which are not me.*"

"I found dose women dere during the expedition. It wasn't a *Spanish* expedition that found da Fountain of Youth. It was a *Swedish* expedition. And it wasn't lookin' fer *The Fountain of Youth* at all. It was lookin' fer *The Lake with Lots of Big Fish*. Anyway, I was explorin' by myself and I found dis lake and went skinnydipping."

"Without your clothes?"

"Janet!"

"Oh, sorry. Of course without your clothes."

"And when I got into the water, I got a tingly feeling."

"And that's how you knew it was The Fountain of Youth? Your body sensed the restorative properties of the water?"

"No, it's because I saw dose two women skinnydipping on da udder side of the lake. It gave me a tingly feeling in my special place."

"Oh Sven, I know that feeling! When I first saw you, I got a tingly feeling in my special place, too!"

"Ya, and dose two women, dey still live dere—in a cabin by da lake. Dey look just as good as dey did 178 years ago. In fact, when I tink about dem it still gives me a tingly feeling in my special place."

"Sven!" said a disappointed Janet. "You can only have tingly feelings in your special place for me!"

"Uf-da!" said Sven. "Dis monogamy ting is gonna be hard!"

"But you're willing to be true to me, right? To share all of your love with nobody else but me, right"

"So..." said Sven, changing the subject, "you're really turning into a zombie, huh?"

"Yes...I'm afraid I'm getting close to the final transition...the one where I'll become a zombie for good."

Janet cried a tear in the shape of a duck. It dripped down her cheek and hit the floor and its splash made the sound of a 'quack'."

"Uf da!" exclaimed Sven, "Den it's a gut ting we didn't made da whoopee!"

"Yes...the danger was too great," Janet said melodramatically, with a far-away look in her eyes, "far too great...extremely far too great...way extremely far too great."

Janet cried a tear in the shape of a cat. When it hit the floor, guess what sound it made?

"Tell me, Sven," asked Janet wistfully, "have you been saving yourself for me? What I mean is...have you ever been with another woman?"

Sven suddenly had a coughing fit.

"Huh?" said Sven when he finished coughing. "Janet, I bin around 178 years, ya? I been wit 485 women."

"But I would have been the best, right?" asked Janet hopefully.

"Well," replied Sven without thinking through the implications, "I tink you woulda been in da top 200."

"Sven!" said Janet, her feelings hurt.

"Oh wait now, I figured dot wrong," said a backpedaling Sven, "You woulda been da best one, ya for shure, no problem."

"Um... should I believe you? Or are you just backpedaling?"

"Janet, I only bin with dose hundreds of women to help me forget about you."

"Sven, that makes no sense at all. All those women were before we ever met."

"So..." said Sven, realizing that once again he better change the subject, "are you scared?"

"Of death? No, I'm not scared of death. The only thing I'm scared of is of not being with you."

"Oh Janet, dot will never happen!"

"Oh, thank you Sven!" said Janet, giving him a big hug. "You've made me the happiest seventeen-year-old girl turning into a zombie in the world!"

Janet suddenly brightened. "Hey Sven, are you up for a walk?"

"Well actually," he answered, "I am laying down in da bed."

"Let's go to Epiphany Meadows!" she exclaimed, holding his hands in hers.

"Uf-da, not *Epiphany Meadows!* Dots da place vere people go to hof life-changing insights and emotional breakthroughs, ya? Whoever goes dere is suddenly face-to-face wit all dere denials and coping mechanisms. Nobody ever goes dere!"

"Well..." said Janet hesitantly, "maybe only people that are running out of time to have an epiphany the old-fashioned way."

"Oh no! We bedder git over dere so we can tie up all da loose plot threads!"

CHAPTER 14

The magical place called Epiphany Meadows was invented by the author at the last minute, when he realized he had no idea how to construct a proper epiphany. He knew that creating a legitimate epiphany would require building up circumstances that force a character to face their denials and coping mechanisms. This would lead to a scene in which the character is impelled to have a *breakthrough*—to dramatically "break through" their psychological resistance—in order to discover the truth. This would require careful plot construction as well as profound knowledge of human nature. It was much easier to invent something called Epiphany Meadows.

Janet and Sven emerged from the cabin into a gloomy afternoon, a cold wind howling from an overcast sky. If the previous cloudy weather symbolized a major plot turning point, this extra-cloudy weather symbolized...or foreshadowed...or whatever the right word is. But in any case, it did it even more.

As Sven and Janet were walking hand-in-hand through the camp, they ran into Aimee.

"C'mon with us!" said Janet, "We're going to Epiphany Meadows!"

"Oh, I really don't need an epiphany!" chuckled Aimee. "As a Buddhist, I already know the truth of my existence."

"Oh, you think so?" said Janet knowingly.

"But I'd like to come along to watch, if that's all right with you two. Will you be consummating your epiphany?"

"Hey Ole," shouted Janet to Ole who appeared suddenly because the author suddenly realized he needed to appear. "When my dad gets here, tell him we all went to Epiphany Meadows!"

"Ya, sure ting!" exclaimed Ole, "Does dot mean dis story is almost goin ta be over?"

"Yes!" exclaimed Janet, "We're leading up to the big finale."

"I have someting to say to Sven," said Ole.

"Ya?" said Sven. "You wanna say goodbye, because maybe you'll never see me again, ya?"

"No. I want you to know I still am against your relationship with Janet."

Well!" huffed Janet. "That's not a very nice attitude."

Turning their backs to the not-very-nice Ole, the three walked beyond camp into the dark woods, sort of like the part in *The Wizard of Oz* when it was Dorothy and the Scarecrow and the Tin Man, except the characters were all different and the setting was different and there was no Toto the dog and no singing.

Soon, they came upon a gate, marked with a sign:

WARNING

BEYOND THIS GATE LIES EPIPHANY MEADOWS

SEVERE DANGER OF LIFE-CHANGING INSIGHTS

Sven opened the gate, and all three entered the meadows. Inside the gate, it was warm and sunshiny. Early morning light cast a warm glow through light mist, like on a Hallmark® card.

In Epiphany Meadows, the sun is always just coming up. It symbolizes the transitions of life. It symbolizes that there's always a new dawn after every sunset, a new chapter, a new beginning.

Disneyland advertises itself as "The Happiest Place on Earth." But Disneyland ain't got nothin' on Epiphany Meadows.

The grassy meadow was bright green, surrounded by tall woody things. Indescribably beautiful red and orange flowers popped from the ground along the trail as they walked by. Birds chirped a happy song, as butterflies burst from cocoons and flittered about in the sunshine.

Even though the birds were hungry they refused to eat the pretty butterflies. They also refused to eat any of the worms that were poking out of the ground, swaying happily at the joy of being alive.

"How can we justify taking another life to sustain our own?" asked one of the birds. "That's not life-fulfilling."

"But if we don't eat," answered another bird, "We'll starve to death. And that's not life-fulfilling either."

Then a nearby blueberry bush said, "Hey birds, I have a bunch of juicy delicious blueberries over here."

The first bird replied, "Hello, blueberry bush. Thanks, but we wouldn't dream of taking any of those blueberries that you did such a good job growing."

"Oh, that's okay!" said the blueberry bush. "I grew these just for you. Later on you'll poop them out, fertilizing them so they'll grow into new blueberry bushes. You'd be doing me a favor, actually."

Janet gazed into the sunrisey sky, filled with puffy clouds that resembled unicorns, kittens, and magical fairy things. Then a bright rainbow appeared, even though there were no rain clouds, which was really weird. Then Janet turned to her two companions.

"Okay!" she said. "Who's first?"

"I'll go first!" said Aimee. "My epiphany is that my Buddhism has been a total sham. I've been using all that 'focus on the present' garbage not as a genuine embrace of the moment, but as a denial of facing my past and fear of making commitments toward the future."

"Wow!" exclaimed Aimee. "That's really profound!"

"Yeah!" said Aimee. "I've totally distorted the legitimate teachings of Buddhism into their exact opposite. Rather than use them to *increase* awareness, I've been using them to *suppress* awareness."

"Oh, I see!" said Janet. "That explains that dopey 'Mona Lisa' smile you always have."

"I'm not even Italian!" added Aimee. "Boy, am I screwed up!"

"Okay!" said Janet. "Who's next?"

"Wait!" said Aimee. "I'm not quite done. I want you to know, Janet, that because of you I realized that my Minneapolis boyfriend wasn't an enlightened Buddhist sage *or* a zombie."

"No?"

"No, he was just an *idiot*. A moron. A typical product of American culture. A zombie in the metaphorical sense: Humanity without a brain, without rational thought. Humanity living on the basest level of physical existence."

"I'm so glad, Aimee!" exclaimed Janet. "It's so awesome that I could help you make a life-changing epiphany. It reaffirms my philosophy of life that the only way to fulfil myself is by fulfilling others."

Just then, Janet's father crashed through the gate behind the wheels of a rental car, and screeched to a stop in the meadow, even though the meadow was grassy.

"Oh, hi daddy!" waved Janet. "We're all having epiphanies. Do you want to go next?"

"Okay," said Janet's father, emerging from the car. "My so-called 'religion' has been a sham. Have you ever researched the life of Joseph Smith? He made it up as he went along! Got horny so he decided God told him it was cool to have multiple wives. My epiphany is that I've been using my focus on Heaven and 'everlasting life' not to make this life meaningful, but to *avoid* making this life meaningful."

"Wow!" exclaimed Janet. "That's really profound!"

"Yeah!" chimed in Aimee, "And such a great counterpoint to my epiphany!"

"Absolutely!" said Janet's father. "I've totally distorted religion to its exact opposite. When you get down to the roots—the core meaning—the only thing that all religions basically want us to do is to *love each other*. But I've been using religion not to *love* everybody, but to *judge* everybody. And judging is the exact opposite of loving."

"Wow!" exclaimed Aimee."

"Oh, that reminds me," added Janet's father, "Sorry, Janet, for implying that you were an alcoholic slut."

"No problem, daddy!" chirped Janet.

"Also," added Janet's father, "sorry for not being there with you at the doctor's office when you got diagnosed with becoming a zombie."

"That's okay, daddy!"

"And for not being there for you, generally speaking, for your entire childhood and early teenage years."

"That's okay, daddy!"

"And for not being there at your birth."

"That's okay, daddy!"

"And at your conception."

"That's okay, guy who is suddenly not my daddy!"

"But I want you to know that I abandoned you just as well as any real father would have abandoned his real daughter."

"I forgive you, guy who is now back to being my daddy!"

At exactly that moment, The Njördsöň Gang ambled into the meadow. They no longer seemed to be the coolest and toughest gang in Lake Wichiganawaneehoohaw Wayward Youth Recovery Camp. They ambled quietly and with great humbleness. If they were dogs, they would had their tails tucked between their legs. If they were cats, they wouldn't have. Cats are stuck-up jerks who lack the ability to be humble about anything.

"We came to share our epiphanies," said Lars, "and maybe throw in some apologies while we're at it."

"Go right ahead!" said Janet.

"We're breaking up The Njördsön Gang. We realized that since humanity is one family, hurting other people also hurts ourselves."

"Wow, what an awesome epiphany!"

"Ya, it sure is. So we are officially disbanding The Njördsön Gang. We's reforming ourselves as *The Njördsön Not-for-Profit Institute to Help People Dot's Be Needin' Our Help.*"

"Way cool!" said Janet. "Okay, who's next?"

"I'll go," said Hulda. "I want to add an apology to that epiphany. Janet, I'm sorry for making those posters and Photoshopping your intelligent head onto the body of a supermodel that's only slightly smarter than a chipmunk."

"I accept your apology!" said Janet.

"And for implying that you have sex with pickles."

"Well," said Janet, "that's a little more challenging, but I accept your apology for that, too."

"I hof an apology, too!" said Hjalmar, "or actually more like a confession. But dis confession I be directing to Sven."

"Oh ya?" said Sven.

"Ya. Sven, I hof a confession to make to you.."

"You do?"

"Remember when you caught us puttin' up dem posters of Janet? And remember when you asked me if it was my idea? I told you that Hjalmar made me do it, remember?"

"Ya, I sure do remember dot," said Sven.

"Well, it wasn't Hjalmar," said Hjalmar. "It was me."

"You lied to me?"

"Ya! But I svear, it was only to protect Hjalmar."

"Well, I guess I forgive you," said Sven, "since it seems to be da ting to do."

"OKAY, WHO'S NEXT?" shouted Janet to the group. "NOW SERVING NUMBER SIX."

"I'm next!" said Ole, who had just scooted into the meadow. If you think that description is leading to some statement about Ole being a good scooter, then you're wrong. Actually, you're right.

"Do you have an epiphany?" asked Janet. "Or perhaps an apology?"

"Or both," added Sven. "We'll take either one or both togeder."

"Hmm…" pondered Ole. "It's not really one or da oder. It's more like an offer of a reconciliation moment."

"What do you think, Janet," asked Sven. "Does that work for you?"

"Sure!" said Janet, "we accept all life-affirming dramatic moments."

"Okay den," said Ole, turning to Sven. "Sven, I haven't been fair to you. I was against this whole relationship with Janet, all because I thought we had some kind of 'bad history' or 'unresolved issues' or something like dot."

"Ya, dot's true," said Sven. "Ever since dot time you chased me with a shotgun, I kinda had a feeling you weren't my best buddy."

"This is so life-affirming, Ole!" said Janet. "So you came here to have a big emotional moment where you cleanse your soul by revealing whatever dark secret you've been holding inside—a secret that was blocking the love in your heart from flowing out of your body into the world?"

"Huh?" said Ole. "No, not really. Da thing is, I don' have any 'history' or 'issues' with Sven. I never did."

"That's it?" said a slightly disappointed Janet. "No drama? No breaking down?"

"Nope."

"Well," sniffed Janet. "That really wasn't a very good one."

"Dot's about is good as it gets for an old Swede, ya?" said Ole. "But Lena is next, and I tink she's got a more better one."

Suddenly, Lena appeared with a more better one.

"Well I sure hope so!" said Janet.

"Oh my dear Janet," said Lena, with much more emotion than Ole was capable of. "Remember back when you had pine needle tea with me and Ole in our cabin?"

"Oh yes!" said Janet. "I'm sorry for killing your houseplant!"

"Oh dot's okay," reassured Lena. "Everting's gotta die sometime."

"That's very profound, I guess."

"And speaking of turning into a zombie, remember when I said I'd love you unconditionally, unless you turned into the same kind of undead flesh-eating monster that killed my real daughter?"

"Yes! That was right after you adopted me as your surrogate mother. How could I forget your complete rejection of me right after you expressed your loving acceptance? Of course, I couldn't tell you that I was turning into the same kind of undead flesh-eating monster that killed your real daughter."

"So in addition to turning into the same kind of undead flesh-eating monster that killed my real daughter, you lied to me!"

"Oh, I guess you're right," said Janet. "That's probably a bad thing, huh?"

"Well, dot's why I'm here right now," explained Lena. "I'm here to tell ya dot I still love you even though you're turning into the same kind of undead flesh-eating monster that killed my real daughter."

"Oh, I love you too, surrogate mother!"

"And that you lied to me."

"Oh, I love you too now even more, surrogate mother!"

Janet and Lena hugged. The aura of emotional warmth and pure joy was overwhelming. The birds all went "Aww!" and the sun burned just a little brighter, even though that was scientifically impossible.

"Thanks, surrogate mother," said Janet. "It felt so good to have that great life-affirming hug."

"Well," said Lena, "I figured we was running out of time to hug. After you turn into a zombie, don't expect too many more hugs."

"Okay, surrogate mother!"

"Or any hugs."

"Hey Janet," said Aimee, "has everyone else had their epiphanies? Because we're coming down to the biggies, the last two that everybody has been waiting for."

"HEY EVERYBODY!" shouted Janet to the crowd. "ANY MORE EPIPHANIES? ACT NOW OR LOSE YOUR CHANCE FOR A LIFE-CHANGING REALIZATION."

"WE'VE ALL HAD OUR EPIPHANIES," said everybody in unison. "SO YOU CAN GO RIGHT AHEAD."

"Janet, we all owe you a huge 'thank you'!" said Aimee. "Because of you all our lives are better. The process of you turning into a zombie has resolved our problems and made us into deeper and more compassionate people. This is a perfect example of your philosophy of life: *The true miracle is in giving, not receiving.*"

"Wrong philosophy," said Janet. "You must be thinking of another dying teenage girl story."

"Well, all I can say is that you should turn into a zombie more often."

"I don't think that's possible," said Janet. "I don't think you can do it more than once. Becoming a zombie is pretty much a one-way journey."

"Maybe scientists will find a cure for zombie-ism? Then when you're back to being human, you can come back and turn into a zombie again. By then we should have a bunch of new problems for you to resolve."

"Hey," Sven asked Janet, "I have a real good epiphany all ready to—"

"Sorry Sven," said Janet. "I'm going to have to jump in here and do my epiphany. Sorry for cutting in! But I sense I have about two minutes left before I make my final transformation into a flesh-eating zombie."

"Oh, dots no problem," said Sven.

"Hey Janet?" asked Janet's father. "What's all this about becoming a flesh-eating zombie?"

"I have no time to explain now, daddy!"

"How about later, after the transformation?"

"Won't work," explained Janet, "because my ability to express myself will become limited to screaming *Must have brains!*"

"Oh, that's alright," reasoned Janet's father, "I'll go back and read this story from the beginning later."

"Thanks, daddy!" smiled Janet, removing the glasses which the author neglected to mention she'd been wearing since the beginning of the story.

"Wow!" said Sven, his eyes widening in surprise. "Without dose glasses, you don't look like a nerd no more. In fact, youse is now da sexiest woman at Lake Wichiganawaneehoohaw Wayward Youth Recovery Camp!"

"Thanks, Sven," said Janet, even though she realized it wasn't much of a compliment considering the competition. "But I'm running out of time for my epiphany. Okay, here goes: What I've learned from facing my upcoming zombie transformation—never knowing moment-to-moment if it would be my last as a sentient, self-conscious being—is that life is precious. Each moment should be lived fully, as if it is our last. Because it just might be! Life shouldn't be saved up for a rainy day that may never come."

"Wow!" exclaimed Aimee. "That's really profound!"

"Yeah!" replied Janet. "In other words, I really should have had sex with Sven when I had the chance. Now I'll never experience a large Swedish member inside my special place."

"Hey," said Sven, "Do I get to haf un epiphany?"

"Wait a sec, Sven," said Janet. "I've got one more epiphany to go. I've been thinking a lot about why I was sent here, why I was being punished for something I didn't do, which led to a lot of pretentious thoughts about whether life—and by extension, the universe—is rational."

"Oh that's right," said Aimee. "You were having that internal monologue in the back seat when I was driving you here from Duluth."

"Yes! And my epiphany is that life *is* rational! It's *not* topsy-turvy or a cosmic knock-knock joke. It was fate that I was punished unfairly, because it led to me being here to have all these epiphanies with all of you. So my final epiphany is that life is meaningful. There is some sort of cosmic 'big picture' even if it's beyond our ability to fully comprehend."

"Is it my turn yet?" asked Sven.

"Sure," said Lena, checking the watch that suddenly appeared on her wrist. "But try to be concise, okay? You've got about 40 seconds before I become a zombie, at which point my ability to be an active listener pretty much goes out the window."

"Oh, no pressure, huh?" said Sven. Suddenly losing his Swedish accent, he continued. "Actually, I have two epiphanies. The first one is: Janet saved my life. She taught me everything about life. About hope. About the long journey ahead. Her love is like the wind. I can't see it, but I can feel it."

"Sven!" said Janet. "That sounds like something from a cheesy melodrama about dying teenage girls."

"I'm just repeating what you said before."

"And what happened to your Swedish accent?"

"Oops! Okay, I got da Svedish accent back!"

"Great! What's your other epiphany?"

"My oder epiphany is dis: People probably tink dot hofing eternal youth is yoost *great*, ya? But dots only if you tink dot life and death are opposite tings. My epiphany is I realize dot life und death are two sides of da same coin, and death is what makes life meaningful, ya? I haf to live with da fact dot everybody I know will die, but I must go on alone...all alone...forever and ever. I have been trapped in a living heck. If only I could find a way to end it."

Suddenly, Janet got a strange feeling. But it was only indigestion. Then she got another strange feeling. Her skin became a gray pallor. Her eyes glazed over. Her IQ dropped by 120 points.

With her last remaining vestige of sentient consciousness, she cried out: "Oh, Sven darling, I think I can take care of that for you!" Then she sunk her teeth deeply into Sven's shoulder.

"Ow," said Sven. Then, his eyes starting to glaze over, added, "Uf-da! At last! I vill be released from entrapment in my own living heck! Now you and me Janet, we can finally be togeder!"

His eyes completed glazing over as his skin turned gray and his IQ dropped only 20 points, since it wasn't that high to begin with.

With his dull gray hand, he held Janet's dull gray hand. They smiled a really gross zombie smile and sweetly growled at each other, then staggered hand-in-hand out of Epiphany Meadows and back into the cold, dark woods.

Janet's father watched them amble off. Suddenly, he realized that he would never see his daughter again, for which the appropriate emotion would be sadness. So he decided that being sad would be a good idea. As he watched, he heard the last words he would ever hear from Janet, as she growled, "Brains!" followed by Sven growling, "Ya, ve must hof brains!"

Janet's father and Aimee remained in the meadow, as everyone else meandered through the gates and out of the meadow with big life-affirming smiles on their optimistic faces.

Janet's father turned to Aimee and offered, "It's kind of heartwarming, in a totally non-heartwarming way. Do you know what I mean?"

"No," replied Aimee.

"Well, it's like this," said Janet's father, beginning to sniffle as if he was about to cry or something. "I'm never going to see my little girl grow up."

"Well, you haven't really seen her grow up so far, so what's the difference."

"Oh good point," he said. "Okay, I'll quit sniffling as if I was about to cry or something. I can only really think of one more thing to say. I've thought deeply about all of this for the past 27 seconds, and do you know the most important thing I've learned?"

"What?"

"Well, actually nothing. But it felt like I should say something profound-sounding at this point."

"What point is that?"

"The End."

~ ~ ~

About the Author

Scott Erickson is a writer of humor and satire. He is a two-time winner of the Mona Schreiber Prize for Humorous Fiction and Nonfiction. One of his stories was included in the book *Laugh Your Shorts Off*, a compilation of contest winners from the website *Humor and Life in Particular*.

He has done some interesting things in his life. He spent 5-1/2 months backpacking around the biggest lake in the world, lived for 1-1/2 years at a rural not-for-profit institute teaching sustainable living skills, and spent a summer helping friends establish an organic farm.

He feels at home in Portland, Oregon, which has the largest roller skating rink west of the Mississippi River and the highest concentration of craft beer breweries in America. He is possibly the nicest curmudgeon you'll ever meet.

More information can be found at
www.scott-erickson-writer.com

Made in the USA
Charleston, SC
10 March 2016